I0763435

THE GREAT PUPPY ESCAPE

(The Adventures of Belle and Bubba)

Book #1

CR HIATT
TK COBB

AMB

Contents

THE GREAT PUPPY ESCAPE I
CONTENTS II
COPYRIGHT IV
AUTHOR'S NOTE V
PROLOGUE: THE DOG RESCUERS 1
CHAPTER 1: NOT ALL HUMANS ARE GOOD 7
CHAPTER 2: YOU WERE BORN WITH GIFTS 14
CHAPTER 3: HUNT FOR FOOD 20
CHAPTER 4: WAS I REALLY PART HUMAN 25
CHAPTER 5: JOEY, THE TALKING BEAR 31
CHAPTER 6: RETURN OF THE DOG TRAINER 39
CHAPTER 7: AREN'T WE GOOD PUPPIES 46
CHAPTER 8: CAUGHT IN THE ACT 52
CHAPTER 9: TELLING STORIES 58
CHAPTER 10: THE MAIDS 68
CHAPTER 11: RETURN TO JOEY 74
CHAPTER 12: WHOA, A LIVE BEAR 79
CHAPTER 13: WE FORGOT FOOD 88
CHAPTER 14: BELIEVE AND HOPE 93
CHAPTER 15: WE CAN DO ANYTHING 102
CHAPTER 16: AS WE GOT OLDER 109
CHAPTER 17: DON'T TAKE MY BROTHER 119
CHAPTER 18: I WON'T LOSE ANOTHER BROTHER 128
CHAPTER 19: TURN US INTO A FREAK SHOW 136
CHAPTER 20: THE ESCAPEES 142
CHAPTER 21: RED POLKA-DOT UMBRELLA 152
CHAPTER 22: ILLEGAL CAR PART FACTORY 160
CHAPTER 23: CHASE OF OUR LIVES 169
CHAPTER 24: CHICKEN COOP IS OUR NEW HOME 178
CHAPTER 25: WE ARE FREE 182
CHAPTER 26: A MIRACLE 188
CHAPTER 27: IS HE A BELIEVER 193

CHAPTER 28: STORES AND MORE HUMANS 201
CHAPTER 29: WHAT'S NOT TO LIKE 208
CHAPTER 30: I HAVE NIGHTMARES TOO 216
CHAPTER 31: IT WAS AN ACCIDENT 227
CHAPTER 32: GROWING UP AND GETTING BIGGER 234
CHAPTER 33: BUBBA GOES TO WORK 241
EPILOGUE 252

Copyright

AMB

First edition, May, 2023
Printed in the United States of America

Author's Note

I originally started Book #1 of this series based on the events of my puppy's early life before she came to live in our home. The story developed into so much more, but was all inspired by her and the other dogs surrounding us. Sometimes, I think dogs really are humans.

“You cannot share your life with a dog and not know perfectly well that animals have personalities, minds, and feelings.”

~ Jane Goodall

Second
Gate
Field
Pond #2
Auto Parts
Field
Field
Pond #1
Dumpster
House
Basement
Frog
Pond
DOG
PORCH
First
Gate
No Trespassing
Guard Dogs

Prologue: The Dog Rescuers

An inflatable police boat cut through the water, sending waves crashing against the sides. The blue and red lights flashed and its siren blared, alerting that help was on the way.

Jared, a young police officer wearing a yellow life jacket, piloted the inflatable toward a motorboat that was currently on fire.

Smoke and flames were shooting up into the sky!

A second officer searched the water through his binoculars.

"We've got two victims in the water just south of the fire, having trouble staying afloat."

"The fire is raging out of control!" Officer Jared said. "We can't take the rescue in too close. We'll need to toss the throw bags."

"Those victims look pretty weak," the second officer added. "They're going to need some help."

Officer Jared turned to look at us, the two rescue dogs on board. "You ready?"

That's me, Belle, and my brother, Bubba, wearing our police life vests. Both of us were equipped with flotation devices, preparing to jump into action once they tossed the throw bags.

We might be young, age-wise, but we know what we're doing. We have been training for this exact type of rescue.

Once the inflatable stopped, Officer Jared tossed two throw bags out into the rough water.

Bubba and I stood up on our hind legs on the edge of the boat, almost as if we were humans, and dove into the water.

We dog paddled toward the throw bags, grabbed the extended rope into our mouths, and carried them toward the victims as if we had been doing this our entire lives.

* * *

Wait, I'm getting ahead of myself. That's not how the story starts.

I know what you're thinking. How could two dogs, still puppies, be trained to do what only humans are normally capable of?

We didn't start out as rescue dogs with human abilities. You won't believe it when I tell you. Nobody does...

I was one of five Golden Retriever Lab-mixed puppies born on a hot summer day in August. The first four males pushed their way out as if they couldn't wait to explore. Three of them were golden, like me. One was charcoal, almost black. He had floppy ears like us, but looked more like the lab doggy daddy, only with longer fur.

Some time passed before I showed up; the only girl. I was number five. The runt of the litter, I was a tiny little thing. But good things come in small packages, so don't hold that against me.

When people think of Retrievers and Lab puppies, they think of cuteness overload.

That didn't happen for me and my siblings. Our early life was... well, without being too graphic, it was dreadful.

Terrifying, really, and we were always too dirty to be cute. We looked like little homeless mutts.

There were only two of us together after that summer. We still have nightmares, occasionally, but only one of us will talk about it.

This is our story...

Chapter 1: Not all humans are good

When I was born, I could open my eyes almost right away. I could see, hear, smell, and understand things going on around me, even human things. It wasn't long before I was moving around, too. Unusual, I know, especially when I was number five, the runt.

I wish it didn't happen that way.

I saw and heard horrible things.

I wanted to crawl back inside my doggy mommy's belly. The world seemed like a scary place.

We lived under a porch in front of a big old two-story apartment house that leaked when it rained, turned the dirt into muddy rivers, and was always cold for days after.

There were several acres that were surrounded by a tall fence and a gate that was always kept shut. A sign that was posted out front said no trespassers, trained and vicious guard dogs on duty.

That might not sound scary to some, but to young pups like us, it seemed like monsters and bullies surrounded us, and there was no way out.

It was always dark and dreary under our porch, even when the weather was nice.

There was no green grass to walk on, and the acreage was like a maze of jungles and junkyards all in one. Clutter was everywhere and the tall weeds and vines that spread like wildfire blocked the sun. There was a huge dumpster, but more junk ended up on the ground than inside.

Old and wrecked cars, trucks, and farming equipment took up the entire left side of the yard near the huge rusted windmill. Various parts and stacks of tires were strewn about from other vehicles taken apart, and the air always smelled like engine oil. The tractors, trucks, and cars that did work were parked in the field out back.

That field was off-limits to us, but we didn't know why.

On the other side of the yard, there was a swimming pond that had frogs living in it. The water was a thick green liquid, but not a pretty green. We could hear them talking to one another all day and all night long: ribbit, ribbit, ribbit.

If we snuck up onto the porch, we heard the waves of the ocean nearby and could see snow-capped mountains in the distance. Various types of birds flew from tree to tree, building their nests, and singing. Woodpeckers knocked on wood. Sometimes the seagulls would fly overhead and talk. Honeybees buzzed around, searching for pollen on flowers that grew on the vines. Carpenter bees drilled holes in the distressed wood on the home and made nests for their queens. Squirrels and chipmunks raced along the top of the fence and electrical wires, but they rarely came inside for fear of the scary dogs.

We also heard children in the neighborhood laughing as they played hide-and-seek, kick-the-can, and when they chased fireflies at night. Teenagers would shoot-the-hoops, and other times, play soccer or football in the street. To us, they all seemed so far away, yet they were just beyond the gate.

At night, when everything was quiet, we would sneak up onto the porch, look up at the stars, and dream. Yes, puppies and dogs have dreams and wishes, too.

There was a big, exciting world outside that fenced yard. But we did not know how to get to it, physically.

Leroy Jones, the human who lived on the first floor of the apartment house, was a wicked, wicked man.

He had long red whiskers down to his chest, and beady black eyes that always seemed to watch us. Every day, he wore overall jeans with a cotton shirt, a straw hat covered his head, and he always carried a pitchfork. When he yelled, it came out as a roar and the earth shook underneath us. He was a big man with a belly that hung out over his belt and he was a mean, old coot.

Nobody knows why. Sometimes, people are just mean for no reason. He was always yelling and swatting at us. We were deathly afraid of Leroy Jones.

Where are those dag-blasted puppies?
Mean Leroy Jones and his vicious guard dogs

Chapter 2: You were born with gifts

One morning, a man just as scary as Leroy Jones showed up. He was the dog trainer who came to see our doggy mommy. She was a Golden Retriever left behind by a former tenant of the apartment building. Leroy Jones was giving her away because he wanted no more puppies around.

When the trainer arrived to pick her up, Leroy Jones also gave him one of my brothers.

I was so upset. I didn't understand why all of us couldn't stay together.

One night before she left, our doggy mommy folded me into her paws while my brothers slept.

"Be strong, little one, and take care of your brothers," she said to me.

She knew she was leaving, but didn't want me to be sad. I peered up at her with an unsure look on my face.

"What do you mean, momma?"

"They'll need you."

"But I'm the runt."

She snuggled me closer. "You were born with gifts, little one. You'll see. You will find a way."

She must have seen things in me I wasn't aware of. I shook my head, worried that I would fail. "I'm just a little girl… I wish I was human, and then I wouldn't be so afraid."

"Do not be afraid, little one," she said. "You can do anything you set your mind to, if you believe."

I nuzzled my head into the fur at her neck as she told me the same story she did the night before, and the night before that.

"*Once upon a time, there was a precious little puppy who thought she was human. She could stand upright on her hind legs and stretch herself tall. She taught herself to walk. Her paws were so flexible she could hold on to things as if she had thumbs. She took her brothers on adventures and used her wits to find food. That little precious puppy could do anything a human could do.*"

As I listened to her words, I imagined I was actually doing them. By the time I drifted off to sleep, I was physically walking on my hind legs with my paws in the air.

At the time of her talk, I didn't know what my doggy mommy was trying to tell me.

Once she and number one were gone, leaving the rest of us puppies without food, I knew what she meant. My brothers were physically stronger than me, but my mind was smart. They needed me to survive, but I needed them, too.

Our doggy daddy was a big black lab that was trained to protect the yard and business. Leroy Jones forced him to be mean and called him Brutus.

Brutus was nice to us when Leroy Jones wasn't looking. Now that our doggy mommy was gone, I could hear him whining at night. He missed her, too.

Two other dogs helped protect the yard. I did not know what type of dogs they were. Somebody must have been awfully mean to them when they were puppies. They were wicked mean now, growling and snarling at us every day, and their teeth were always showing. They were bullies and always tormented us. We tried to steer clear of them.

It was our own Cinderella story, only we were puppies.

Chapter 3: Hunt for food

Now that our doggy mommy was gone, I had to come up with sneaky ways to find food each day. Leroy Jones always fed his guard dogs, even Brutus, but he left us to fend for ourselves.

Sometimes Brutus would hide some of his food, and then I would sneak over to get it later. That only worked out when Leroy Jones was not watching.

It seemed like he was always watching. And the punishment was usually worse than the crime.

One morning, I rushed through the maze of weeds and vines, trying to dodge the scary bullies. I could see them wandering around, with their snouts in the air, trying to track my scent. I kept low to the ground, underneath the vines that gave off an odor which confused them. One of them almost caught up to me at one point, but I got away when he got his paw caught in a rat trap.

Since I was so small, I could see those and knew to avoid them. I don't know why Leroy Jones put out traps when he had two vicious dogs to keep the yard clear of rodents. I assumed it was just another way to scare us.

Today, I was in search of scraps in the dumpster. Leroy Jones finally took out his trash. Gross, I know, but some days that was all we could find. During my hunt, I discovered a broken window that led to a basement underneath the apartment house.

The next day, I made the trek again and hid in an overgrown bush until Leroy Jones and the two bullies disappeared out back. When I was sure they were out of sight, I pushed my way through.

THUD!

The drop was further than I expected. I fell on top of an old chest and hit my head.

It dazed and confused me for a few seconds. When I finally snapped out of it, I felt a small lump on my head.

A loud noise suddenly echoed throughout the large room, causing the walls to shake and me to shiver in fear.

"What was that?" I muttered to myself.

At first, I thought it was Leroy Jones. It was so loud the floor underneath the chest vibrated, just like when he yelled. But he was out in the field and nobody else lived at the apartments. I sat up on my hind legs and let my eyes adjust to the darkness.

And then I saw it: a big monstrosity that looked like a scary monster with eyes and a mouth, but no nose, hiding in the corner. Long arms came out of it and went up into the ceiling, but they weren't like human arms or doggy arms. They were big and wide and looked scary in the dark.

My eyes went wide when its big mouth suddenly opened, and it looked like it was spitting fire.

The floor shook again, and the noise followed.

"Get. Out!"

At least that's what it sounded like. My mind was probably just hearing things, because the mouth closed up again and it got eerily quiet. I have been imagining a lot lately. You would too if you lived with Leroy Jones and the bullies.

Chapter 4: Was I really part human

Instead of running back out the window, I forced myself to stay. I needed to see if Leroy Jones stored any food in the basement. Maybe there was a second refrigerator, or canned goods stacked on shelves. My brothers were hungry, and I was determined to find them something to eat. Since I was the smallest, I could hide from the guard dogs easier than they could. Plus, I discovered I could use my paws, just like in my doggy mommy's story.

Was I really part human? Is that why I could understand things that my brothers couldn't?

I jumped down off the chest and nosed around the basement. The floor was all cement, cold and damp. As I wandered, I kept the monster in the corner of my eye.

With every step I took, it felt like there were other eyes watching me, too.

I had a great sense of smell, and my hearing was better than a human. If there was somebody else in the basement with me, I would know it. I just couldn't shake the feeling. It had to be the monster that was making me feel uneasy.

I studied the room. There was no second refrigerator. There were shelves built along one wall that had plastic bins on them. Huge metal toolboxes and a work desk stacked with papers took up the space along another wall. The area behind the monster had cardboard boxes, stacks of books, toys, stuffed animals, and a collection of dolls dressed in different outfits. One looked like a weather girl, dressed in a yellow raincoat with a red polka-dot umbrella clasped in her toy hand. Another looked like an adventurer with camping equipment and an inflatable boat. There was also a bedroom set for a little girl. Why would Leroy Jones have a child's bedroom set and toys?

I did not see any canned goods or any food at all, which meant I would have to sneak inside the kitchen while Leroy Jones was out in the field.

The stairs leading up to the main floor were in the center of the room. The monster was still opening its mouth and making noise, but I tried to ignore it as I approached the steps. I couldn't let fear stop me.

From the bottom, I looked up at the door. It seemed so far away, like a long, dark tunnel that went on for miles. I slowly ventured up the old wooden steps and stopped to listen when I reached the top.

Hearing no sounds, I instinctively stood up on my hind legs, placed my paw on the knob, turned it, and opened the door.

OMG!

You're probably thinking the same thing I was right at that moment. When did I learn how to do that?

My doggy mommy's story was coming true! I could stand upright and use my paws as if I had thumbs! And I seemed to get much taller.

After I took a moment to get over the shock, I stuck my head inside the kitchen. Leroy Jones had not returned, but he would soon. I hurried into the room and looked around.

It was just as messy inside as it was in the yard. It smelled like something was rotting. Trash and scraps of food from his past meals cluttered the table and counters. Dirt and muddy boot and paw prints covered the floor, obviously from Leroy Jones and the bullies.

Behind all the trash and grub on the counter, I spotted the bag of food for his guard dogs. If I grabbed a few handfuls, he wouldn't even notice. There was a plastic grocery bag on the table. I grabbed it with my teeth. At the counter, I stood up on my hind legs again, scooped out some food with my paw and dropped it into the bag.

I hurried back down and opened the refrigerator. There were leftover bones from one of his meals, so I grabbed those, too. My brothers would fight over them, but number four usually refereed. He would convince them to share.

Holding the bag of food in my mouth, I hurried back down the stairs and closed the door behind me.

"Those were some fancy moves you made getting into that kitchen," a voice said when I reached the bottom step, and it scared the life right out of me.

I froze and dropped the bag of food, terrified. "Who said that?"

Chapter 5: Joey, the talking bear

Was the monster speaking to me?

I saw movement out of the corner of my eye and looked through the opening of the stairs. That's when I noticed a brown teddy bear wearing a camouflage uniform among the stuffed animals on the shelves. One of its paws was waving at me.

I blinked several times. Maybe getting hit on the head was making me nutty. How could a stuffed animal be waving?

"You're not imagining things," the teddy bear said. "That's me."

So that's who was watching me. I wasn't imagining it. Since the bear is not real, there's no scent.

"You can talk?" I said, surprised.

Without warning, the teddy bear jumped off the wooden shelf and walked toward me on its own two paws, making me take a step back from the shock.

"So can you," the teddy bear responded.

"And you can walk?" I added, when the bear stood right in front of me.

"Give the puppy a medal for stating the obvious," the teddy bear mocked.

I shrugged. "I have brothers; I understand sarcasm."

The teddy bear put its paw out. “Name’s Joey, the army bear, but you can just call me Joey.”

I offered my paw. Even before I could stand on my hind legs and use my paws, I knew how to shake and give a high-five. I do it with my brothers all the time.

“I don’t have a name, but you can call me number five.”

“You can talk and walk too, number five,” Joey said. “We can do anything when we believe we can.”

My eyes went wide. “My doggy mommy said that.”

“That must be where you got your smarts from.”

“So why do they call you Joey, the army bear?”

“Hello,” he mocked. “Don’t you see the uniform?”

I shrugged. “You’re not a soldier, so what’s the reason a teddy bear is in a camouflage uniform?”

Joey used his right paw and pointed toward a button on his other paw. “I was a gift to a little girl whose daddy is in the army. If you push the playback button, you’ll hear his voice speaking to her.”

I pushed the button and heard a male voice. "Hi Hayden, it's daddy; I'll be home soon. I love you."

"Where is the little girl, and why aren't you still with her?"

"The mother and daughter used to live in the second-floor apartment," Joey said. "Mean Leroy Jones raised the rent and kicked them out when they couldn't afford it. He locked them out so they couldn't take their things. I got left behind."

"That's so cruel," I said, madder than ever. "I bet the little girl is missing you and all her toys."

Joey looked sad. "Yes, I've been trying to get to her, but I can't."

"Why not? You can walk," I said, and then I remembered. "You mean because of the locked gate?"

He shook his head. "Not just that. The yard is like the Amazon jungle. When it rains, it's like a river. Even when it doesn't, the air is so humid. If I get wet, the message for Hayden could get ruined."

"Oh." I had to think about that one. "So you're stuck in here?"

"I'm trying to come up with another plan," he said, trying not to be negative.

"What's that ugly monster over there?" I asked, while contemplating Joey's problem.

"That's not a monster," he said, laughing. It was funny. His little belly jiggled when he laughed. "It's a heater that keeps the place warm. This is an old apartment building with old things in it."

I sighed. "Well, it looks like a monster," I said, defending myself. "It has eyes and a mouth, and says scary things when it opens its mouth and shows red flames."

This time, Joey was on the cement floor, rolling around and laughing. "Oh, that is hilarious. You are too funny."

"I'm glad I could amuse you."

I was about to get serious and talk about his problem, when BANG! A loud noise shook the house and freaked us both out.

And then another BANG!

"That's mean Leroy Jones slamming cabinets," Joey said. "You better get going. Sometimes, he comes down here to work with his tools."

Joey jumped up off the cement floor, waddled as fast as he could and climbed up the shelves, returning to his place with the other stuffed animals.

Looking at him now, I would never have guessed he came alive just a few moments ago. He blended in with all the other stuffed animals on the shelf.

Chapter 6: Return of the Dog Trainer

I gathered up the bag of food and the pieces that fell out. I didn't want any evidence left behind.

By the time I climbed back out the window, I knew something scary was going on out in the yard. Brutus was pacing the yard, as if there was an unwanted visitor, and the mean dogs were ferociously barking at him.

As Joey said, scurrying through the weeds and vines was like running through the Amazon. The air was humid from the heat and moisture leftover from the rain, and the sun never made its way through to give me light. I was running blind. The leaves and branches continuously whacked me across the face. The consolation was that it kept me hidden from the bullies. Thankfully, their attention was currently on something else.

When I made it back under the porch, my brothers were huddled together, shivering.

"What's going on out there?" Brother number four asked me when I joined them.

"I don't know," I said. "But our doggy daddy is not happy."

Seconds later, a dark shadow suddenly appeared above us. We were so scared; we pushed ourselves further into our hiding place.

Loud, angry voices followed. Two humans were arguing.

I peeked out from underneath the steps. The dog trainer who took our doggy mommy was arguing with Leroy Jones.

"You still owe me money from those parts I gave you," the trainer bellowed.

"I don't have it yet," Leroy Jones responded. "I'll pay you when the buyer comes."

"When will that be?"

"A few days, maybe."

"Then give me another puppy."

"You already took one when you picked up the mother dog."

The scary man looked toward the porch. “Well, I want another one; and then I’ll call us even.”

Leroy Jones’ lips curved into an evil grin and he scratched the side of his whiskers.

I scooted back with my brothers when the dark shadows completely covered our hideaway. Two pairs of eyes looked down at us.

“I knew you mutts would come in handy,” Leroy Jones uttered, as his smelly hand reached toward us. It smelled like car oil and gasoline.

Brutus barked at Leroy Jones. “Get away from them,” was what I heard him say, but all Leroy Jones heard was barking, because he’s not a believer.

"Lay down, Brutus," he yelled at him, using the mean tone that even scared Brutus.

Before we could do anything to stop it, Leroy Jones snatched brother number two and swung him around toward the trainer.

"Take him," Leroy Jones said. "He's useless to me, anyway."

"Good," the scary man responded. "They make excellent guard animals when you can train 'em young. The older dog will take longer."

I gasped. I understood what the human was saying. He was training our doggy mommy and brothers to become mean guard dogs.

Bullies.

This can't be.

"He's only a puppy," I yelled. "He needs his brothers and sister."

But the scary man didn't understand or care what I was saying.

Brutus was barking really loud now. He was so upset. Leroy Jones rapped his pitchfork against the wood deck several times. The loud sound made everybody jump, even the guard dogs.

"Get in the house, Brutus, and lay down until I tell you to come out," he yelled.

When Brutus hesitated, Leroy Jones marched toward the door and opened it. "Now!" he added.

Brutus knew he couldn't refuse. He hung his head toward the ground as he walked toward the house, ashamed. He glanced back at us one more time with a forlorn look in his eyes and then disappeared inside.

BANG!

Leroy Jones slammed the door shut behind him. Brutus could sneak out of the doggy door, but he wouldn't dare.

Chapter 7: Aren't we good puppies

After the dog trainer left with our brother, Leroy Jones and the bullies returned to the field again. I don't know what was out there, but it was the only area he paid attention to in the yard.

With them gone, I knew we had a few moments, so I gave my brothers the bag of food. I had to keep up my strength too, so I took a few bites for myself. When they discovered the bones, they didn't fight over them as they usually would have. They were too upset. Having our brother taken took the fight out of them.

They huddled together and nibbled on them half-heartedly. It made me so sad. While they were occupied, I snuck up onto the porch and went inside the doggy door to check on Brutus.

He was lying on a dusty blanket with his head flat on the ground. I'm just a puppy, but I could tell he was very sad. Our doggy mommy was gone, and now, so were two of our brothers.

I kissed him on the forehead. "You still have us, daddy," I said. He put his paw on me, as if it was a hug.

"You better get back out there, little one," he said. "If you get caught, Leroy Jones can be plenty mean."

Wicked Leroy Jones.

I scooted back out through the doggy door, making sure the wicked man and his two bullies were nowhere around.

"Why is he giving away our family?" brother number three asked when I returned. "Aren't we good puppies?"

I snuggled them close, like our doggy mommy did. "Of course we are good. We can't control what happens, but we can control how we react. We have to think positive. Maybe the scary man will feed them better than Leroy Jones does."

Brother number four smirked as he looked around at the junkyard we were living in. "At least they're out of this rat trap of a place."

"Will the dog trainer teach them to be mean, like the bullies?"

Number four shook his head. "Our doggy mommy and brothers already have the good in them. No mean dog trainer can change that."

"That's right," I said. "Like Brutus. They trained him to be mean, but he is still nice to us when Leroy Jones is not looking. He knows the difference."

To help them fall asleep that night, I told them about the talking bear I met in the basement. They didn't believe me. They thought I was just making up another fairy tale to get their minds off of our brother. To be honest, I was a little animated with my story.

When they finally drifted off, I cried myself to sleep. Now, I only had two brothers. And a sad doggy daddy that had to do what Leroy Jones made him do. There were other thoughts going through my imagination too, like how to escape from the dismal environment we were trapped in, but I had to think those through.

Chapter 8: Caught in the act

For the next few days, there was a lot of activity in the yard, which kept me from returning to the basement. Leroy Jones had special visitors coming and going, looking at things in his special field. But the odd thing was; they never came through the front gate. How did they get in?

The dog trainer was among them, which had me worried he was there to take another puppy.

Leroy Jones chained Brutus to a metal post, so the bullies were left in charge of watching the perimeter. That meant if they cornered us, Brutus couldn't protect us.

I tried to keep my brothers under the porch and out of sight. It was horrifying when they went out and the bullies tormented them. I could usually hear them coming, so I would run or hide. My brothers felt different. They didn't want to run away or hide.

"We're no cowards," number four said to me one day. "We have to be tough and fight back. It's not fair that we're always stuck under the porch while the bullies have full use of the yard all day."

"You're right, it's not fair. But the bullies are so much bigger than you, and vicious. One bite could really hurt you."

"I would rather get hurt than hide."

That statement made me proud they were my brothers.

One afternoon, I thought Leroy Jones was out in the field with his friends. I hurried through the maze of weeds and vines and snuck in through the doggy door, hoping to sneak more of the dog food. It wasn't good for our tummies to always eat scraps or dumpster food. If my brothers were determined to go up against the bullies, they needed to build some muscle.

I was up on my hind legs, using my paws to gather it into the plastic bag, looking almost human, when the wicked man unexpectedly walked into the kitchen and caught me. He had to have been spying on me and chosen that moment to surprise me. If I hadn't been rustling the food bag, my ears would have heard him.

"Well, what do we have here?" he said, pulling on his whiskers with a wicked smirk on his face.

I jumped back away from the counter, only to be trapped in the corner of his cabinets trying to hold on to the bag of food. I was terrified, and he knew it.

His beady black eyes stared at me as if he just won some big prize, and he was trying to put a scheme together on how he could cash in.

"Imagine the money I could make off of you," he finally said, with a snarky grin. "People would pay enormous sums of money for images and videos of a puppy doing human things."

Was he threatening to exploit me? That didn't sound good.

"Hmmm, I wonder if the other dogs have your abilities. I bet the charcoal-colored one does. You don't think I see the two of you sneaking around for food, but I do."

See what I mean? He's always watching us.

He rubbed his whiskers again. "You two might just be the payout I was hoping for. You are just young puppies now, but I bet those skills get better as you get older. I'll be able to stop working so hard to make a buck. You might even make me rich."

His sudden joy at my expense made me nervous. What does he do out in the field that makes him money, anyway?

"Go on, get back to the porch!" he said, rubbing his hands together as those crazy ideas were forming in his head.

Miraculously, he let me go without punishment and let me keep the food, but only because he had men waiting for him out in the field. When I returned to my brothers, I was afraid our lives had just taken a bad turn, all because he caught me in the act.

I couldn't say that to them. They would get upset. Instead, I set out to teach them how to use their imagination to escape in their minds—like I learned to do.

Chapter 9: Telling stories

There was a stump underneath the porch from an old tree cut down before we were born. One afternoon, I sat on top and pretended I was a human librarian reading from a book.

"I'm going to read you a story," I said to my brothers. "I want you to imagine it is real, and when you go to sleep at night, believe it and pray for it too."

I saw the skeptical look in their eyes as they tilted their heads from side to side, trying to understand.

"*Once upon a time, there were three puppies who thought they were human...*"

"I don't want to be human like mean Leroy Jones," brother number three interrupted with a frown on his puppy-dog face.

"We are nice humans who live with a wonderful family," I responded. "They feed us and love us, and take us on adventures?"

"What adventures; what do we do?" he asked, suddenly curious.

"We can do anything humans can do," I said.

"Where do we go?" number four said.

"Anywhere we want to go."

"Can we play in the ocean, like the one beyond the fence where the sound of the waves put us to sleep at night?"

I smiled. "It just so happens, our human family is taking us to the beach today."

"That's just your imag-in-ation," number three said, stuttering when trying to say the big word.

"Yes, but if we imagine it, believe it, and pray on it each night, it could happen."

Number three smirked. "No, it won't. We're not that lucky."

"Maybe we have to make our own luck," I said. "Let's try it."

My brothers looked at each other and shrugged, but only because they didn't understand. Or maybe things were so bad that they didn't think it could hurt.

"Today, our new human family is coming to pick us up," I said in an animated voice. *"They open the locked gate and we step outside to freedom. Butterflies and dragonflies greet us as they fly from*

flower to flower. Oh look, there are hummingbirds too!"

"The squirrels, bunnies, and chipmunks, which normally avoid Leroy Jones' yard because of the traps, are out in the open gathering food.

Birds are chirping, welcoming us outside. Children are laughing and playing in their front yards, urging us to watch.

After a while, we hop into our new family's truck with our beach body boards and drive to the ocean."

My brothers' eyes were suddenly wide in amazement at the visual scene I described.

"We know how to body surf?" number three asked.

"Remember, if we believe, we can do anything the humans can."

"*The beach is packed with children and adults running and laughing. Dogs are chasing balls. Kids are building castles and swimming in the water. We line up on the sand with our boards. The water splashes over our paws as waves crash into the shoreline. It is icy cold at first, but we don't mind. On the count of one, two, three, we rush into the ocean. Once we're in the deep end, we flop down onto our bellies to catch a wave.*"

From the smiles on their faces, I could tell they were finally imagining the scene as if it was real. They could visualize it and feel it.

"*We whip this way and that through the salty water. We're no longer afraid. The bullies can't get to us. Our ears flop up and down as the breeze blows through our fur. The water splashes our puppy faces, making it hard to see. But we don't care, because we're free.*"

"Yes," number four said, pumping his paw into the air, caught up in the excitement of my tale.

"*Number four gets so excited he stands upright on the board, and surfs the waves, using his paws to balance.*"

"No Way," number three said. "That's so cool."

"*We follow the waves to the shore, shake the water off and roll around on our backs, the way we like to do.*"

"But we will be covered in sand and get in trouble," number four said, worried about the punishment if Leroy Jones found out.

"*Our nice human family won't care how dirty we get,*" I said. "*And then we make a sandcastle and watch the other dogs and kids play.*"

And suddenly, with no warning: BOOM! A loud noise from inside the house echoed in our ears and interrupted our fairy tale.

Chapter 10: The maids

I stopped telling our imaginative tale and rushed over to huddle with my brothers. Our minds immediately returned to our dismal reality.

We heard Leroy Jones shove the door open and stomp down the porch steps.

He looked furious when he stuck his face down under the porch. His dark eyes glared at us.

"Which one of you useless mutts snuck inside the house and left the muddy paw prints?"

"Here we go again," number four said, rolling his eyes and not caring if he got in trouble.

This was happening a lot since Leroy Jones caught me standing upright and using my paws.

"It wasn't us, you mean human," I said. "Ask your precious guard dogs."

He didn't understand a word we said.

His gigantic hands reached under the porch and snatched me and number four by the fur on our necks. Our other brother shivered in fear, and backed into the corner, afraid for us and afraid of the bullies.

"Stay hidden until we get back," I yelled to him.

"Get in there and clean up the mess," Leroy Jones said, following us and pushing us through the door.

Inside, we saw the messy kitchen and muddy floor.

"The bullies made the mess," number four said.

"He knows," I responded, annoyed. "They do it every day."

The prints were clearly left by bigger paws than ours, and they left all their trash behind, as usual.

Leroy Jones smirked and handed us small uniforms, a mop, brooms, and rags. "Earn your keep, for that nice porch you sleep under."

"I'm sorry I taught you how to stand upright," I said to my brother.

"Maybe it will come in handy when it's time to bring down this yahoo," he responded.

Ever since our doggy mommy told me that story—and I imagined it to be true—I was consistently standing upright and using my paws. I assumed any dog could to it, if they practiced, so I taught number four. Now, he helps me sneak food when number three is still asleep. He just can't use his paws in the same ways I do. Even though I'm the runt, my paws are huge. My doggy mommy said having enormous paws was a sign that I was going to be big and beautiful, like her.

Sometimes, we waited until Leroy Jones and the bullies were asleep, and then we crawled through the doggy door. Since they were slobs, we always found leftovers on the table and counters. Most of it was yuck, but once in a while we found a hamburger from a place called Mackie Ds. We corralled the edible stuff. Now that number four was helping me, it was easy to sneak in and out with one of us as a lookout. We were as quiet as two little mice who knew how to avoid the traps.

After Leroy Jones discovered our human abilities, he had been using us as his own little housekeeping service. Though, I don't know why. He and the bullies usually made a mess minutes after. I think it was just to torment us. We had to wear masks; it smelled so bad inside.

Once we had his silly uniforms on and started cleaning, he took pictures of us with his phone.

"Nobody believes me when I tell them two puppies clean my house," he said with his mean laugh. "Now, I've got the proof."

I stuck my tongue out at him underneath the mask. Four must have sensed it. He put his paw up for a high-five.

Leroy Jones didn't get the joke.

Chapter 11: Return to Joey

My chance to return to the basement finally arrived. This time, I took my brothers with me. They were convinced a talking stuffed teddy bear only came from my vivid imagination.

Leroy Jones and the bullies took a ride on the tractor out back in the field. Doing what, I don't know. The diesel noise was so loud we could hear them and would know when they were returning. Brutus would also bark to let us know.

All things being considered, it was a good day for an adventure. The sky was blue. The sun was shining, even though we couldn't see it when wandering through the maze of vines. At least it was brighter. We could hear the gray catbirds nibbling on the berries from the taller vines, where the dogs couldn't reach them on a normal day. And the squirrels were walking across branches, searching for acorns and nuts to bring back to their own hideaways.

Number three was fascinated by all the bugs crawling across the dirt. The bees buzzed in and out of the vines, stopping now and then to check out some sweet-smelling nectar of a flower miraculously growing without sun.

Since he hadn't learned how to use his hind legs yet, he would remain outside, as a lookout, to watch the window. I just hoped the insects didn't distract him from his job. Even though we could hear the tractor, the bullies might decide to return before Leroy Jones did.

This time, I was careful climbing through the window and helped number four to do the same. I warned him about the long drop and the heating system. He still got scared when it opened its mouth, and he saw the red flames.

"So where is this talking bear you keep talking about?" he said, looking around. "I still say you made it up."

"Joey!" I called out.

All I heard was the noisy sound from the heater. I walked over toward the stairs with my brother following. He wouldn't admit it, but I could tell he was just as scared of the heater as I was. Even though I knew it couldn't hurt me, it still looked like a big ole monster.

"It's safe, Joey," I said, walking closer to the shelves of toys. "Leroy Jones is out in the field."

I looked toward the stuffed animals. There was no brown teddy bear. "He's not here," I said.

"See, I told you it was just your imagination," my brother said, smirking.

"It wasn't my imagination. He was right here!"

I stood up on my hind legs and moved the toys around, thinking he got stuck behind one of them.

When I couldn't find him, I scratched my head and wondered if number four was right. Maybe when I bonked my head, my imagination went a little crazy. But that couldn't be. I know it was true. I spoke to him. He laughed at my fear of the heater.

Then I got worried. Did Leroy Jones find out about him and lock him up somewhere?

Chapter 12: Whoa, a live bear

I looked over at the dollhouse and checked to see if Joey was hiding inside or behind it. He reminded me of number four; I could picture both of them playing pranks on me.

I sighed, frustrated, and then busted up laughing when Joey suddenly appeared out of nowhere and tapped my brother on the shoulder.

Number four nearly jumped three feet in the air.

“Whoa!” he said, stunned at the sight of an actual stuffed teddy bear coming alive in front of him.

“I see your brother is not a genuine believer, like you,” Joey teased.

My brother’s eyes were enormous. He circled Joey, trying to see if what he was seeing was actually what he was seeing. “Impressive.”

Joey winked. “I aim to please. Though, I don’t think a talking stuffed animal is that much different from two Retriever puppies who think and act like humans.”

“She believes she’s human,” my brother said, motioning toward me. “I’m just an overachiever.”

Joey laughed. “And a modest one, too.”

"Some hangout you have here," my brother said, checking out the toys, dolls, and other stuffed animals lined up on the shelves. "Do they come alive too?"

"Nope, just me."

"Why?"

"Why what?"

"Why you, and not them?"

Joey shrugged. "I guess they don't believe."

"Sorry I couldn't come back sooner," I said to Joey. "Leroy Jones and his bullies have been watching us constantly."

"Yes, I know," Joey said. "He has been coming down here a lot, too. I don't trust him."

"Me either," I said. "He discovered my brother and I have human abilities and he is scheming to exploit us for money."

Joey frowned and put his paw to his chin as if he was thinking. "That's not good... but I have a plan."

"A plan for what?" my brother asked.

I glanced at my brother. "Don't you remember? Joey was a gift to a child from her father in the military. They used to live in the apartment upstairs before Leroy Jones kicked them out. Joey is trying to escape and get back to the child."

"How do you know where the child is?"

"They live with the child's grandmother," Joey said, recalling the address from his memory. "111 Cranberry Lane."

"So what's your plan?" I said, curious.

"We can help each other," Joey said. "If you and your brothers protect me from the weather elements, I can help you escape from Leroy Jones. There is another way out of here, besides the locked gate out front."

My brother and I looked at each other. Our eyes were filled with a glimmer of hope.

"How?"

He motioned us over toward the work desk by the tools. "There's a map mixed up with those documents on the desk. Well, it's more like a blueprint of the property."

Number four got down on all fours so Joey could use him as leverage to get up on the desk. He was a lot smaller than us.

“If we take the map, mean Leroy Jones will notice. He comes down here all the time. We need to study it, and come back on another day if we have to, until we have it memorized.”

Standing up on my hind legs, I leaned over the desk and viewed the document. “Is the terrain that difficult to remember?”

“For us little folk, it’s a lot farther than you think,” Joey said. “Haven’t you ever wondered how Leroy Jones leaves the property without opening the front gate? How do his friends and workers suddenly show up?”

“The scary dude that took our doggy mommy away showed up without the gate opening,” number four said. “I wondered how he got in without us seeing him."

"Yes, now that you mention it," I added.

Joey placed his paw on a section of the map. "There is another gate beyond the field. It's a lot of land to cover. They use the tractor to get around."

"That's why he won't allow us near the field," I said, looking at my brother. "He doesn't want us to know about it."

The three of us studied the map, trying to plan out the easiest trek from the house to the open escape location. There were many obstacles; the weeds, trees and vines, the rows and rows of parts and vehicles.

"There are also two bodies of water, like ponds or something that we'll have to work our way around," Joey said.

He was right. We wouldn't be able to memorize it in one shot, especially since I could hear the diesel tractor on the move.

A minute later, number three leaned into the basement window. "Uh oh, Leroy Jones is on his way back. I didn't hear him ahead of time. He's coming in hot and the dogs are mad. Sorry."

"Time to go," I said.

Mean Leroy Jones and his bullies returning on the tractor.

Chapter 13: We forgot food

Joey wasted no time. In a flash, he jumped down from the desk and returned to the shelf. I think he was more afraid of Leroy Jones than we were.

Number four stared at the shelf of toys and stuffed animals, and tried to make out which one was Joey. If it wasn't for the camouflage, he looked like all the other brown bears lined up along the wall.

"Guess he's got a lot of practice at doing that," my brother said as we hurried toward the window.

"We'll be back, Joey," I said, as I waited for number four to get through the window and then scooted myself out.

Number three was already running through the weeds and vines, with us following his four paws. He was on a different path than the one we normally take when searching for food. That worried me. I didn't know what obstacles we would run into.

We were cutting it close. I could hear the diesel sound not too far away. I turned around to see how much time we had.

The tractor was close enough for me to see Leroy Jones' beady black eyes. The bullies were pacing in a trailer being pulled by the tractor, barking ferociously, almost as if they knew we were hiding from them. Maybe they could smell us.

"Number three, stop," I yelled out, suddenly, when I turned back around and spotted the heart-shaped leaves of a vine that are covered with stickers and thorns.

When he kept going, I realized he didn't hear me. He was steps away from getting injured when I lunged for him and tackled him off to the side.

"What'd you do that for?" he yelled, aggravated, but also because he feared we would get caught by the tractor closing in on us.

I pointed toward the thorns. "If you get those stuck in your paw, you won't be walking for a few days. Plus, your yelp would alert the bullies."

"Oh, well, thanks," he said, looking sheepish. "I guess I don't get out much to know the right way to go."

"That's okay," I said. "I'll lead us from here. We just need to get over to the other path where the vines have certain odors that will help to keep the bullies away."

"Well, you better get a move-on," number four said. "Those dogs are coming up on us pretty fast."

Sure enough, I looked through the weeds to see the guard dogs leaning over the sides of the trailer, salivating, ready to jump off. But less than a few seconds later, I heard Brutus up ahead the other way, alerting us he was ready. Our doggy daddy was watching out for us.

"This way," I said to my brothers. Instead of pushing our way through the stickers and thorns, I guided them through the tall vines that attached themselves to the house. They were less dangerous and offered a sweet flower for the bees, wasps, or yellow jackets that kept me company on my early morning treks for food. I had taken the path so many times I could probably run it with my eyes closed. There was nothing to cause us harm along the way.

We finally made it to our shelter before the bullies jumped off the trailer and made their predatory rounds.

As we huddled in our little corner, gasping for air, number four glanced over at me. "Um, hate to be the bearer of bad news," he said sheepishly. "We have to go out again. We forgot to search for food."

"Oh, no... just give me a minute to catch my breath."

I flopped down on my belly to rest for a minute or two.

Chapter 14: Believe and hope

Number four and I were eager to start the planning part of our escape. Since we didn't have the map memorized, we didn't want number three to get excited yet. It could take a while before we got the chance to sneak back into the basement.

Instead, I opted to get back to our daily routine of teaching them how to use their imagination instead of making fun of it.

"Today, our new family of humans is teaching us how to drive motorized cars," I said in an excited voice, as if we were already enjoying the adventure.

Number four raised his head up from his nap and eyed me with skepticism.

"We can't drive," number three said in his usual negative mode.

"Remember, we can do anything humans can. Like I keep reminding you, I want you to imagine it, believe it, and then pray for it, and before you know, you can do it."

I told the story in the present tense, as if we already knew how. That was the best way to get them excited enough to believe. At least, that was how it started for me. I listened to my doggy mommy's story, imagined it to be real, believed and prayed. When I snuck into the basement for the first time, I was physically doing what she discussed.

Number four was slowly coming around. I taught him how to get upright. He had been sneaking out with me and getting more adventurous with each trip. Now, I needed him to help me convince number three that it was possible.

But Number three was stubborn. He needed to learn the mindset that we could do anything we dreamed of in our heads. We just had to believe. I encouraged them to follow along as I narrated the adventure.

"*We met up at the park and practiced driving our new cars.*"

"Cool," number four said, trying to show me he was involved. "What color is my car?"

"What color do you want it to be?"

"The same color as the ocean."

"I don't believe in all of this, yet," number three said. "But if it ever happens, I want purple."

I laughed. "Happy to see your enthusiasm," I said. "It is our imagination. Our cars can be whatever color we want them to be."

"Where am I going in my purple car, if this was real?" he asked.

"*We can go anywhere we want, but today we're driving along the streets of our cheerful town. It has cute little stores, and a diner with outdoor dining called Mackie Ds. They have the best hamburgers. Humans and other pets are lined up on the sidewalks and waving at us as we drive by. It's like our own little welcoming parade.*"

"After our drive, we park at the diner and order anything we want to eat from our cars."

"We don't have to go inside?" number four said.

"Nope."

Number three was still hesitant to believe. Even though four did his best to help me encourage him, we couldn't force it. I noticed the hint of a smile, though, when I described us driving through town.

"What adventure are we having tomorrow?" number four asked.

"Tomorrow, our new human family is taking us up to the mountains," I said. I pointed toward the view beyond the gate.

"The snow?" number three said, giving me a sideways glance that revealed his continued skepticism.

"There are no limits to where we can go and what we can do," I said. "Once we're outside that big, scary gate, we can do anything. We get to enjoy all the seasons and all the fun we want. We're going to snowboard, surf the waves, go camping, and ride bikes."

"Really?" number four said with enthusiasm because he wished it was true.

"How can a dog snowboard?" number three asked, looking at me as if I had lost my marbles.

"Just like we did on the body board, only we use our hind legs," I said.

"That was fiction," he reminded me. "We didn't really body surf in the ocean, and four didn't surf the waves. It was just one of your fairy tales."

I sighed and shook my head, disappointed. "It won't work for you if you're always negative."

He shrugged. "I'm a realist."

"We can do anything we set our minds to, and not just in our stories. Our new human family will teach us."

"We don't have a human family! Don't you get it!" he said, revealing his sadness.

He turned his back on us and walked into the corner, plopped down on his belly, and pouted.

I glanced at number four, not knowing what to do.

"Let me talk to him," he said.

I nodded as tears welled up in my eyes. I couldn't get mad at Number three. I know how he hated our life. I wish I could make it better. Right now, all I could do was try to make him feel better using his mind, but he was not as easily convinced. As he said, he was a realist.

His mind was locked in our dismal reality.

Chapter 15: We can do anything

Number four sat down next to number three and placed his paw on top of his head.

"You're not mad at our sister," number four said.

"Of course not; I'm mad at our disgusting situation. What she's talking about is nothing but dreams, and a hopeful fairy tale."

"She's just trying to create a fantasy world for us, so we can have a little pleasure to get us through the day, even if it's only in our minds. It helps me."

Number three peered up at him. "It does?"

"Yeah, it gives me something to hope for."

"But it's not reality."

"Do you enjoy our reality?"

Number three smirked. "What is there to enjoy? Every day, you two are off searching to find us something to eat. If it wasn't for the leaky faucet, we'd be drinking out of the dirty pond and probably get sick. We can't even throw a ball around and have a little fun, for fear of the bullies taking a chunk out of our hides."

"That's what sis is trying to do for us, bro. She's filling our heads with the possibilities. She's trying to show us there is an exciting world out there that we can experience if we just try to imagine it, believe it, and pray for it, and ultimately search for it."

"Do you buy into that?"

"I sleep better at night, knowing it could happen," number four said.

"I could use a good night's sleep."

"I didn't think I could stand upright like the humans do until she taught me, and I followed through with believing it. Now, I can. If I can do that, why couldn't I surf or snowboard?"

"Do you think I could learn to stand upright, too?"

He nodded. "I do. C'mon, let's try it."

Number four glanced over at me and smiled. Then, he got up on his hind legs, like I taught him to do, and used his paws to balance.

"This is how we get the food off the counter," he told number three.

"Number three, I want you to believe we have a new human family who loves us and they're teaching us to do it all. Right now, they are only stories, but if we imagine it, and believe, it could happen."

He frowned, but his tone was better than before. "We're not humans."

"No, but we can do human things, if we believe, and practice."

Four and I finally convinced him to put the negativity aside and at least try it. The two of us practiced standing upright, going slow, so he could watch our technique.

I got on top of the tree stump and pretended it was a snowboard. I positioned myself upright on my two hind legs and balanced with my front paws out to the sides.

"See," I said to him. When four joined me on the stump, I saw three's eyes light up at the possibilities.

"Okay, so maybe there's something to it," he said, though he wasn't convinced.

Reluctantly, he tried it. At first, he struggled. It was a new technique for him. He kept falling off the stump. But we worked at it all day until he felt comfortable.

By bedtime, all three of us were standing upright, smiling, and balancing our paws.

"We can do anything, as long as we believe," I said.

After a few seconds, the two of them repeated the statement: "We can do anything, as long as we believe."

Sadly, when we woke up in the morning and our horrible reality was still the same, number three looked dejected all over again.

I tried to explain. It's not like rubbing a magic genie and our wishes come true. We have to keep working at it and have hope.

"I understand your fears, three," I said to him. "I fight them every morning of every day. It is difficult to be patient and hope when we live with wicked Leroy Jones and the bullies."

Number four nodded his head in agreement. "Bro, it would be easy to give in to the fears, and just be a couple of mutts under Leroy Jones' thumb, but we would hate ourselves if we did."

"I guess," he said.

"We will become stronger and happier if we fight for what we want," number four added.

I nodded. "That's why we imagine it, believe it, and pray for it when we go to bed at night. Hopefully, someday, our dreams will come true, even if it means we have to work to make it happen."

Chapter 16: As we got older

As the days went by, we were getting older, and maybe a little taller, but we had no meat on our bones. Leroy Jones started cracking down on our sneaking around for food. He hid the bag of dog food so we couldn't find it, and just to be mean, tossed the leftovers into a trash barrel.

We knew he was toying with us, wanting us to beg for food. On one occasion, we were so hungry and desperate; we did. He said sure, as long as we posed for pictures so he could make money off of our abilities. The situation was getting dire, and we knew something was going on that we weren't aware of.

Men in suits started showing up. They came through the back gate and walked right up to the door, demanding Leroy Jones show them what was in the field. They would hop onto his tractor-trailer and take a ride. The mean dogs would bark really loud and we would scurry deeper into our hiding place.

Since I had such good ears, I heard everything that was going on, even when they were out in the field. Sometimes, I could hear before anyone else. I didn't always understand, though.

I just knew Leroy Jones was doing something bad.

We did not know how much time had passed, or how old we were. The nights were colder, so we knew summer was over. But the hours and days blended into each other.

The children were no longer playing outside at night like they did during the warm days. We could still hear the birds and see the squirrels searching for nuts, but not as much.

Every day, my worries increased. My brothers needed proper food. The only thing keeping us going was our desire to escape, and the possibility of what we imagined coming true. But how long did we have to wait?

It seemed like forever since we viewed the map, but we haven't been able to get back down to the basement. Sadly, I was losing faith in my imagining technique, even though I urged my brothers to continue.

My hope was dwindling. Maybe it was because I was weak from the lack of food. I couldn't say it out loud, but some days I worried we might never escape.

One morning when Leroy Jones was inside, and it looked like the bullies were napping, I snuck toward the gate and started digging a hole with my enormous paws. I dug as deep as I could and covered it with hay when I noticed the bullies moving around. That night and going on into the next, I waited and watched, hoping for another opportunity to return and continue digging. I kept it a secret and didn't tell my brothers. I didn't want to get them all excited if the plan fell apart.

A rain storm started two days later and dampened my spirits. That would only make the digging that much harder. I don't know how many days passed before the weather cooperated and I finally got another opportunity. When the hole was finally big enough for us to crawl under, and hopefully, dig to the other side, I hurried back to get my brothers.

There were three reasons I knew it could be dangerous: 1) I didn't know what was on the other side of the gate if we could dig our way out; 2) One of us could get trapped in the hole, and 3) The bullies and Leroy Jones could catch us.

My desire to escape and get my brothers to safety urged me to continue.

"C'mon, you two. I dug a hole for us to attempt an escape. We need to go now."

Number four stared at me, stunned. "What about Joey?"

"Right," number three said, nodding his head in agreement. "We can't leave without Joey."

"We promised," number four added.

I hung my head in shame. "I know. I just don't know how much more of this we can take. We're getting older, but we're not growing. I feel so weak, I'm sure you do too. And I'm losing the hope we worked so hard for."

My brothers looked at each other with concern in their eyes. I was normally the one encouraging them to believe. And now it was me who was the one losing faith.

Then it was as if they were channeling my earlier resolve and determination. They huddled close and wrapped me in their paws.

"That's because you took on the burden of taking care of us," number three said.

"Now, let us do some of the work," number four added in a stern, big-brother voice.

Number three said, "We can't leave without helping Joey."

"You would be very sad, if we did," four added.

I knew they were right. I would never forgive myself if we left without helping him.

"I better go fill in the hole then, so the bullies don't find it."

"We'll help you and watch your back," number four said.

We looked toward the area where the bullies usually hovered and didn't see them. I assumed they were back in the field. But once we got close to the gate, we realized we were too late. The bullies discovered the hole and started barking to alert Leroy Jones.

Brutus heard the noise and bounded over, ready to protect us. When he saw the hole, he started digging to make it appear as though he was the one trying to escape. His ploy didn't work.

Leroy Jones already knew the truth.

He had a scowl on his face when he appeared with a shovel. "You thought you'd escape, did you? You worthless mutts don't appreciate how good you've got it. Well, I'll teach you a lesson you won't soon forget."

He re-buried the hole with dirt, packed it down hard, and stormed back into the apartment house, leaving us to wonder what he planned to do.

"I'm sorry, we should have listened," number three said back in the safety of our hideaway.

"Yes, we should have gone with you the minute you told us," number four said with regret.

"Obviously, the bullies were secretly watching," I said. "We would have been caught either way."

Fearing the worst from Leroy Jones, the three of us snuggled close for the rest of the night. Would he lock the doggy door so we couldn't sneak in for the unhealthy scraps? Would he shut the dumpster lid so we couldn't get into the trash? He already hid the bag of dog food. What more could he do?

All we could do was say a few doggy prayers, and ignore the hunger pains in our tummies. Little did we know, the punishment would be worse than we imagined.

Chapter 17: Don't take my brother

I woke up early the following morning. The punishment hadn't been handed out yet, and I was starving. My brothers would be too. While they were still asleep, I hurried along the path I normally take to look for scraps. We had to get something in our bellies. When we were thirsty, we could drink water from the outdoor water spout that leaked. It was just underneath the porch, so it was within reach for us. But we couldn't survive without some food. Anything would do at this point.

When I came upon the vine with berries, I was relieved. Finally, a bit of luck came my way. The berries would be something healthy that wouldn't hurt our tummies. It was also disheartening. If it was the season for berries, that meant it was fall, but how late into fall? We had been living in the dump for a while now, but I couldn't dwell. I needed to get back before my brothers woke up and came looking for me.

"Look, berries," I said to them, trying to inject a little excitement upon my return. "They're growing on the vines, so there will be plenty when we can't get inside the house for food."

They wiped their sleepy eyes and opened their paws. We took our time eating them. One thing we learned from being starved was that you get sick when you finally have food and you eat too fast.

"Leroy Jones chained Brutus to the post again, but he didn't punish us yet," number four said. "What do you think he's planning to do?"

"Maybe he forgot," number three said, feeling hopeful.

"I don't know what he plans to do to us, but let's try not to stress about it," I said. "I'll make sure he knows it was me. I'll clean his house until it's spotless if I have to. I'll let him take his stupid pictures of me so he can sell them to make money."

Number four laughed. "You'll be cleaning all day. He and the bullies mess it up right after it's clean."

"They do it on purpose."

"Are you feeling better today?" number three asked me. "Do you want to tell us one of your stories?"

I smiled at my brother. I knew he was trying to please me. "That's okay. I know you don't like my stories."

He shook his head. "That's not true. I wanted to hear about us going to the mountains."

"I want to hear it too," four said, trying to encourage me.

"Okay." I smiled and took my seat on the tree stump and told them my imaginary tale about us going up to the snow. For several minutes, at least, we put our horrible reality in the back of our minds and dreamed we were on top of the snow-capped mountains, enjoying the fresh air.

"*We carved our way down the slopes, slicing through the fresh powder. All three of us wore colorful snow gear, with helmets and goggles to protect our eyes from the glare of the sun.*"

I suddenly heard a voice that was all too familiar coming from the direction of the field. I stopped reading and froze.

"What's wrong?" number four said.

"I hear someone?" My ears were much better than theirs at hearing things.

"Who is it?"

"Shhhh," I said. I scooted over next to them and wrapped them in my paws.

Footsteps came closer.

Without warning, Leroy Jones reached down and grabbed number three. My brother was bigger than me, but he started shivering in fear.

Puppies have sharp teeth, so I bit Leroy Jones in the hand.

"Ow!" he snarled. "Get away from me, you dag-blasted dog!"

He tried to swat me, but I scooted out of his reach.

"No," I screamed. "Don't take my brother."

He handed him over to the dog trainer. Number four and I rushed out and attacked the trainer's ankles.

"Leave our brother alone!"

Leroy Jones tried to kick us away, but even though we were weak, we were still fast enough to move out of the path of his boot. His belly always got in the way.

Suddenly, his bullies bounded toward us, growling, with their teeth showing. Brutus started barking too, but he was chained to the post. We had to get back to our hiding place before we became the bullies' next meal.

"See, it didn't do me any good to dream," was the last thing I heard number three say, and it broke my heart.

"I'm sorry!"

Number four and I had to put our paws over our ears to avoid hearing our brother's cries.

Leroy Jones laughed as the dog trainer took him away. "That's what happens when you try to get away from Leroy Jones."

I burrowed myself further into the corner. I wanted to be alone. My dreams weren't working out at all. It was my fault number three was taken. If I didn't dig that hole, we wouldn't be punished.

People don't think dogs understand, but I do. Maybe because I wished I was human, but I understood everything. We were a family. If they took our mommy doggy, or one of our brothers, they should have taken all of us. Why couldn't we stay together?

"We won't ever see number three again, will we?" number four asked me, his voice quivering.

"I don't know," I said, feeling worse than ever. I could only hope that he went to be with our doggy mommy and our other brothers.

"I hope he feeds him well," number four added.

That night, I didn't have the heart to pray, fearing that I was the one causing all these bad things to happen.

Chapter 18: I won't lose another brother

As much as I tried to stay positive, I was failing. After losing number three, I thought there was no hope, and that we'd be stuck in this dismal life forever. I dreamed, believed, and prayed every day, but bad things kept happening.

Number four could tell how despondent I was. He took over the story-telling, hoping to get me excited again.

It wasn't working.

Our doggy mommy was gone, and so were our three brothers. One of them was my fault. Would they try to separate me and number four, too? I couldn't let that happen.

"Maybe you weren't clear about your wish," number four said to me unexpectedly after his story failed to inspire me.

"What do you mean?"

"You can stand upright and use your paws. You also talk and think like a human. You have feelings, but you don't know how to control them when you're sad, or how to put them to good use."

I stared at him, trying to comprehend what he was trying to say. But seeing the worried look in his eyes, I finally understood.

"You're right. And now I'm wallowing and feeling sorry for myself."

"Then snap out of it," he said. "Bring back the sister whose stories and imagination made me think I could do anything. You gave me hope that we'll see our doggy mommy and brothers again."

I tried to shove the negative feelings aside. I could see it in his eyes; he needed me to be strong. I couldn't let him down.

"Okay then, number four, let's not wait any longer," I said to him, trying to call upon whatever strength I had left.

"What do you mean?" he said, perking up.

"We need to put our heads together and figure out how to outfox Leroy Jones and the bullies. And get back down to the basement. We need to memorize that map, and figure out how to carry Joey out of there without subjecting him to the elements, and this time, escape for real. When we're free, we will look into finding our doggy mommy and brothers."

"Now that's what I'm talking about!" four said, excited. "Good to have you back, sis."

"We can't just sit back and do nothing while Leroy Jones allows his dog trainer to turn our family into vicious guard dogs. And we can't let them separate us!"

"It's you and me," Number four said. We bumped our paws together.

"I saw some things in the basement that we could use to help us escape," I said with a renewed sense of vigor.

"So, how do we do this without getting caught?"

We huddled close and put together an escape plan.

"The Great Puppy Escape," he teased, trying to keep things light.

We also had to be patient and pay attention to what Leroy Jones and his bullies were doing before we put our plan into action.

For a few days we hid under the porch steps behind the weeds, but watched the yard through an opening in the stairs. We mentally calculated the wicked Leroy Jones' daily routine.

Then the day finally arrived when I knew we had to act.

Leroy Jones had a few work buddies over, discussing something of importance. The dog trainer was one of them, and I just knew they would separate us if we didn't get out of there.

The men sat in chairs by the dirty swimming pond, chatting as if it was a luxurious lake, instead of a body of water filled with frogs and algae. Brutus was still chained, but the bullies walked the perimeter, from one side of the yard to the other. Their evil eyes always darted toward the porch to see if we were sneaking out for food.

"With Leroy Jones hanging out by the pool, he won't be able to see us if we leave," number four said.

"It's the bullies we'll have to watch out for," I said, tracking their perimeter walk from one end to the other. "The weeds and vines will keep us hidden from their view, but if they get a whiff of our scent, they'll come after us."

"We will not let that stop us," he said, feeling a moment of bravery.

"Normally, but remember, we haven't eaten an actual meal in days," I reminded him. "We're weak."

He put his paw up to stop me from being negative. "We're also more determined now than ever before."

"Yes, we are," I agreed. "I just needed to remind you of the danger."

"I'm well aware, sis, but there is more danger for us the longer we stay here."

He was right.

I grabbed the plastic bags I took from inside Leroy Jones' kitchen on a previous food search.

"Then let's do this!"

Chapter 19: Turn us into a freak show

As we prepared to leave, I noticed the tone of Leroy Jones' voice had changed in the discussion with his friends, so much so, it caught my attention. In one breath, he sounded animated and full of excitement, and then his tone altered to maniacal and devious.

He was scheming.

"Seriously, how much cash do you think I could make on those puppies with their human capabilities?"

"Big bucks," someone said.

"Maybe they could do circus acts or something? You saw the pictures... those two dogs were standing upright and cleaning my house."

"Hold up, for a minute," I said to my brother. "Leroy Jones is talking about us right now."

"What's he saying?"

"Hold on." I felt like I was going to be sick. Leroy Jones was getting serious about turning us into a freak show by exploiting our human capabilities.

I listened and re-positioned myself so I could see who he was talking to. It was the dog trainer. Of course, he would be a part of it.

"If you do it right, you could make some serious cash and never have to bother with all that illegal stuff you've got out in the field," the dog trainer said.

"No joke?"

"But I'm talking even bigger than a circus if you get some PR here. They could model pet attire for product sponsorships. Possibly a book deal, maybe an animated movie based on the book or even their own TV series. I could help with the training."

"Wouldn't that be something?" wicked Leroy Jones said, scratching his whiskers with a Cheshire cat grin on his face. The man never grinned or smiled in a friendly manner. He's not only wicked; he's greedy.

"I could set up a meeting," the trainer said. "They will want to come here to see the dogs, so try being nice to the dogs to get them to cooperate. Feeding them would be good. And clean up the place."

"When could you set that up?"

"Right away, just say the word."

Leroy Jones found a scheme where he could put our abilities to profitable use for himself.

"We really have to go," I said, angrier than before and eager to get away, more than ever. "Now."

"What's going on?"

"Leroy Jones is getting serious about exploiting us," I said. "The dog trainer is setting it up."

"No way," four said.

"Joey better be ready to go," I said. "This is our last shot."

The two of us rolled around on the ground under the porch until our fur was coated in dirt.

"To ward off our scent," I said when he gave me a strange look.

"We look like a couple of ruffians," he said.

"Even better for what we're doing."

I took one last look at the hideaway where we were born and spent the early months of our lives. Good riddance.

We each put a couple of plastic bags in our mouths, waited until the bullies were on the other side of the yard, and then quietly left our birthplace. As we entered the path of weeds and vines that I used to get to the basement window, I prayed it would be the last time.

Chapter 20: The escapees

"You should take the lead," I said as we started off. "You know the path just as well as I do, since you helped me sneak into Leroy Jones' house searching for food."

We were both good with our noses and sniffing out trouble as if we were trained. But my sense of smell, hearing and communication abilities were more enhanced than his, only because he was easily distracted. It was better that I watch out for the bullies behind us.

While we moved along the path, my mind drifted back to our early days, after our dog mommy was taken away. I wondered why I picked up on the human traits so easily, and then could teach them to number four. Did it really come down to us being believers? We were walking along the path, both of us on our hind legs, just like humans. We could talk and understand each other. So could Joey the bear, and my doggy mommy and daddy. Leroy Jones and the dog trainer could not understand us. Maybe Joey was right: you can do and be whatever you want, as long as you believe.

Leroy Jones and the dog trainer definitely were not believers.

"Don't forget to stop at the berry vine up ahead," I whispered.

While he nosed his way forward, I kept my ears alert and watched our backs.

Through an opening in the weeds, I noticed the bullies marching the perimeter and unexpectedly halt. They put their snouts up to sniff the air and then turned in our direction. Noses-to-the-ground, they charged our way.

"Oh, no!" I cried. "They got a whiff of our scent. They are coming this way."

"What do I do?"

"Dive under the skunk vine. They hate the smell."

"Which one is the skunk vine?"

"It has white and pinkish flowers."

"Duh, I'm colorblind."

"Then let your nose find it; it stinks."

Sure enough, a hundred yards ahead, he dove under an invasive plant. Its stems were long and the many leaves kept the sun from reaching the other plants underneath.

“Gross,” my brother said.

We huddled together on the ground and let the stinky leaves cover us. I could hear the bullies approaching. Shadows appeared just above our heads. We didn’t dare move. Hopefully, neither one of us was allergic to the plant. We’d be mincemeat if we sneezed.

I peeked out through the leaves. The bullies paused just a few feet from our location. They stood still, listening, and sniffing the air. Their heads whipped from side to side. Searching. Their teeth showed and drool dripped from their mouths.

Along with the skunk, there was a mixture of weeds and vines that gave off various aromas which I hoped would hide our scent.

The bullies were so close.

I glanced at my brother. We were so afraid of being caught. The idea of going back to the porch, stuck here forever, was not an option.

We remained perfectly still. My body felt like it was going to explode. My heart hammered in my chest. I finally breathed a sigh of relief when their noses finally reached the skunk vine. I could visibly see them react and physically retreat away from the smell. After a few seconds, they gave up and marched back in the gate's direction.

"That was close," my brother whispered.

"We were about to be exterminated."

We stayed there for a moment longer until our heart rates calmed down. Once we were sure the bullies wouldn't reappear, we continued on our journey.

At the blueberry vine, we loaded up. That was the best we could do until we escaped the yard. I assumed we could get water along the way. The directions on the map showed we would have to go through a section of the field. There was a sprinkler system that probably leaked, just like the faucet under the porch. If not, maybe the pond wasn't as dirty as the one by the house.

After we gathered the berries, I heard voices. I placed a paw on my brother and we watched through the weeds. Leroy Jones and the dog trainer were headed toward where they had Brutus chained.

"You'll need to lock Brutus in the fenced-in area around the chicken coop," I heard Leroy Jones say. "He acts up when I get close to the pups."

"He is their father. It's natural he'd want to protect them," the dog trainer said.

"I don't care," Leroy said. "If you get those film and publishing people to show up and see the pups' abilities, I can't have Brutus interfering."

"You should have taught him to respect you, instead of just yelling," the trainer said. "Dogs respond in certain ways, depending on the tone of your voice."

Leroy Jones frowned. "I ain't got time for that. That's why I pay you to train 'em."

The trainer approached Brutus. I could hear him growling. I saw his teeth. The dog trainer grabbed what looked like a remote from his pocket. When he pushed a button, Brutus stopped barking and complied. He was afraid.

The trainer unlocked the chain, grabbed Brutus by the collar, and ushered him to a fenced-in area with a wood building inside.

"You'll like it in here," the trainer said. "You got the place all to yourself. Those other dogs can't get in."

Brutus didn't fight it. Either he was scared, or liked that he was getting away from the bullies. He was also sad, because he knew we were trying to escape, and he couldn't help.

"Are we just going to let them lock him up?" my brother whispered.

"He's better off in there right now. Once we've escaped... I don't know, but we'll do something. We're no good to him as long as we're also prisoners."

Brutus sensed the despair. He curled up in the wood building and put his head on his paws. I could see his sad, brown eyes all the way from where we were.

"We will be back, doggy daddy," my brother mumbled.

My brother took the lead once again while I kept alert. I couldn't help but glance toward Brutus now and then. He looked so sad.

That was part of the mental struggle I endured since I imagined being human. Aside from the deplorable conditions we had been living in, I was also dealing with an emotional dilemma and identity crisis. I physically looked like a golden retriever, but I was just as comfortable with my human attributes. Since when do dogs have emotions and feelings?

I had better hearing and a sense of smell than humans, but I had feelings about things that dogs weren't normally capable of. My brothers didn't have to deal with the same issues I did. Well, number four sometimes did, but not as much; maybe because he was a male. Brother number three finally learned to stand up on his hind legs when we taught him, but he didn't care about learning other human traits. It was only me and number four. I didn't have an answer for that, but maybe it was just because we wanted it more.

Chapter 21: Red polka-dot umbrella

By the time we finally made it to the basement window, the sun was disappearing behind the trees. Maneuvering the distance between the porch and the window took longer than we planned. To two puppies, it really was like walking through a jungle. The humidity was high, but the air turned cooler and a foggy layer of moisture settled over the yard. Thankfully, my brother and I planned for that.

We crawled through the window, relaxed our paws for the drop onto the chest. Even though we weren't putting on much weight because of our lack of food, we were still getting taller. The fall was no longer hard on the noggin when we landed.

"Four, gather the items we discussed," I said.

My brother jumped down onto the cement floor and followed the instructions we planned out. We knew we had to hurry to make up for the time we lost being cornered by the bullies.

I stared at the shelves of stuffed animals, but couldn't see Joey.

"Joey, there's no time to waste," I said, ignoring the monster's angry noises. "We're getting out of here now, so stretch your weary paws and get ready to move."

"That's dope!" Joey said, popping his head up behind the doll house.

"Dope?"

"It means cool," he said, jumping down from the shelf. "Sheesh, have you been living in a barn? All the kids are saying it."

"Not a barn," I reminded him. "Just under a porch."

"Oh right. I was worried you changed your mind or that mean Leroy Jones fed you to the bullies."

He met up with me by the desk. The map was in the same place, which meant Leroy Jones had no clue we had been looking at it. "We don't have time to study the map. I'm taking it with us."

"He'll know," Joey said.

"Then we better get far enough away that it won't matter if he finds out."

When I gathered the map, there was a picture of the dog trainer's facility underneath it, showing the kennels in his yard. I grabbed that too.

"It is cool that we're finally ready to skedaddle, but aren't your forgetting something?" Joey said to me.

Right then, number four returned with the items. "Stand still for a minute, Joey," he said.

Joey gave him a strange look when he noticed the umbrella and raincoat that he disrobed from the weather doll.

"You're wearing the coat and carrying the umbrella. They will protect you from any rain or moisture and keep the message safe for Hayden."

"Dude," Joey said with a smile from ear to ear. "That's ingenious, really. You're not just strong and handsome like me, number four; you've got a brain too."

"No," four responded. "You're right about me being strong and handsome, but my sister is the brains. She told me about the umbrella and raincoat."

I shrugged. "I don't think the weather doll will miss them. But Leroy Jones might notice a red polka-dot umbrella missing from the shelf. We better put some distance between us and the house pretty fast."

Number four tossed me some clothing that he had taken from the dolls. "We might need to stay warm in the elements.

There's no meat on our bones to keep us warm."

"Good thinking."

We hurried into the shirts and pants, and forced some stretch doll shoes onto our paws.

"In case I forget to say it later," Joey said. "Thank you for bringing some happiness back to Hayden. She used to listen to the message from her daddy before bed each night."

"Alright, let's stop dawdling with all this sentiment," my brother said. "Let's get outta here."

"Your brother didn't get the human trait called feelings, did he?" Joey teased.

Number four scoffed. "Feelings won't help us if we get caught trying to escape."

"Touche."

I helped my brother tuck Joey's paws into the sleeves of the raincoat and buttoned it. His tummy was bigger than the dolls, so it barely covered his hips. We couldn't get the hood to cover his round head either, so we used the rain hat that was stuffed in the weather girl's pocket. And then we ripped the plastic bags in half and tied one around each of his paws to protect them from getting wet.

Joey waddled around in circles for a moment. "I feel like a mummy."

"Okay, mummy, let's go," my brother said, getting anxious.

I held onto the map and picture of the doggy kennel where our doggy mommy and siblings were, and climbed out the window.

Joey couldn't jump in his little yellow raincoat, so number four helped him up, and then I pulled him out through the window.

"Whoa, so this is what the outside world looks like when you're planning the great escape," Joey said, looking around. "It sure ain't Oz."

Chapter 22: Illegal car part factory

From where we stood, all we could see were the weeds and vines, and a glimpse of the field. There were tractors, trucks, cars, and a good mile's worth of automobile parts that Leroy Jones had stored out back.

"I think wicked Leroy Jones has an illegal car part factory out in his field," Joey said.

"What makes you say that?" I asked.

"One day, I heard a bunch of commotion, so I hoisted myself up to the window. It was at night, so hard to see, but he had his tractor lights on. Men were unloading parts off of a big truck into the tractor-trailer and carting them to the field. Besides, what other reason would he have to keep all those vehicles and parts and keep the front gate locked every day, with vicious dogs patrolling?"

"You're probably right. I heard the dog trainer say what he was doing was illegal. You're pretty smart, Joey."

"I've got it all," Joey teased. "Brawn, brains, and handsome as well."

I smiled. It was good to have a little levity during such a stressful time.

Once my brother was back outside, we ran in the field's direction to make up for the lost time.

The weeds and vines seemed to grow taller the further away from the house we were, so we walked in single file. Maybe Leroy Jones grew the vines to hide what was in the field. We didn't dare take the path that the tractor normally took. The bullies would see us for sure.

We ran into a problem right away. We had only been walking for twenty minutes, but we had to stop every so often to help Joey catch up.

"I'll fix this," my brother said. "Climb aboard, Joey. If we keep stopping, it'll take us a year to escape this crazy place."

My brother put his paw out to lift Joey up around his neck. It was funny. With my brother standing upright and a round ball of fur behind his head, he looked like a father carrying his son to see the fireworks on the 4th of July.

"Thanks number four," Joey said. "I don't want to be the reason we're delayed."

"No problem. You're shorter, and have to move twice as fast just to keep up is all. I got this!"

I let my brother take the lead again and we settled into a silent rhythm for a long while. We wouldn't admit it out loud, but each one of us was too distressed to carry on a conversation.

It was scary.

We knew the seriousness of what we were doing. We feared even a whispered conversation could echo through the yard and get back to Leroy Jones, which would alert him to the discovery that we were gone. Once that happened, he and the bullies would be on the warpath. In Leroy Jones' mind, nothing was going to stand in the way of showing the world he owned dogs with human abilities.

Freak show, indeed.

"See that steel post up ahead?" I said to my brother. "We need to veer left there. Then you'll need to blow up that inflatable so we can get across the small pond. That should take us to the stone wall where the sprinkler system starts. We can take a brief rest, have some berries, and get some water. Then we'll continue from there. We'll have to cross another big pond after that. The exit is not too far from there."

* * *

Meanwhile, after Leroy Jones said goodbye to his friends, he decided he would take his dog trainer's advice. He went inside his house, grabbed two plastic bowls from his cabinet, and loaded some of the bullies' dog food into the dishes. He added the leftover gravy from his refrigerator on top.

"Those dag-blasted dogs better appreciate this," he said to no one in particular. He carried the dishes outside and marched toward the porch. His two bullies followed.

He lowered himself down and slipped the bowls underneath the steps. "Here ya go, mutts. Hope you appreciate my dogs sharing their food with you."

He stood back up and motioned the bullies to follow him into the shadows. The puppies wouldn't come out of their hiding place as long as he or his dogs were nearby.

After waiting several minutes, he lowered himself down so he could see under the porch. It was late, but it wasn't pitch-black, because of the motion-detector lights. If those mutts were under there, they should have come out by now. He knew they had to be starving. Yet, the food was still untouched.

“Brutus,” he yelled. “Where are those dag-blasted dogs of yours?”

Brutus stood up, ears alert and his tail out. He was stuck inside a chicken coop, so what could he do?

“They better not try to escape again,” he muttered to himself.

His two guard dogs started pacing the perimeter of the yard, getting ready to go to work. Their mouths were salivating at the thought of finally catching their prey.

Leroy Jones glared at them. “You didn’t alert me that there was a problem. Get out there and find them!”

Sensing danger, Brutus started barking, loud, to send the alert that trouble was coming.

Chapter 23: Chase of our lives

The three of us sat on the ground with our backs to the stone wall, taking a moment so my brother and I could enjoy the berries and quench our thirst. Joey didn't need food or water. Before we ate too many, I closed the plastic bags to save some for later and we resumed our trek.

An anguished bark broke the silence. It was so loud it hurt my ears and caused me to jump up in a panic.

"Did you hear that?"

"That's Brutus," my brother said.

"He's alerting us to trouble."

"C'mon Joey, climb aboard."

Everything moved fast now. We knew Brutus' alarm meant the bullies were tracking. Now that I was paying attention, the pounding of their paws on the ground echoed in my ears. They weren't close yet, but they were coming.

"Run," I yelled.

We took off, moving as fast as our paws would carry us. With Joey holding on for dear life, my brother led us back into the maze of vines. The angry breathing of the bullies was getting closer.

We weaved in and out of the rows of vines, trying to keep them off track. We were involved in the chase for our lives. The bullies were bigger and madder than ever because we got away. They knew they would be punished by Leroy Jones if they failed.

Number four readied the inflatable and tossed it into the edge of the big pond. The three of us hurried inside and started rowing with the sticks we found, pushing us away from the land. The bullies would have to come into the water to get us. I didn't know if they could swim.

It was getting darker out, making it hard to see. Up in the distance, I noticed a glimmer of light.

"What is that up ahead?"

"Maybe it's the clearing," my brother said.

"If so, the exit is just beyond the pond," I said, feeling a measure of hope that we might make it.

"We got this, sis."

"Hurry!" I yelled when I heard the panting dogs coming up behind us.

A few minutes later, the inflatable made it to shallow water. My brother stepped out and carried Joey out to safety. I saw him rush through a specter of light in the weeds until they made it out to the clearing.

I was gathering the map and bag of berries, and that's when I realized it was fireflies lighting the way for us to go.

"Keep going all the way," I yelled to my brother.

I stepped out and walked upright toward the edge, still viewing the map to make sure we were close.

"The exit gate is right next to a lamppost."

"We made it. I see the gate," my brother shouted a few moments later.

I breathed a sigh of relief. All he had to do was go out to freedom.

Then, I heard GROWLING! So close, my fur stood on end.

One bully was right behind me. The second one was suddenly right in front of me, teeth showing and ready for the battle of vicious dog versus puppy.

I couldn't go up against a bully that was much larger than me, physically, so I had to be smart. I stepped back out of his reach to give myself a moment to think. Before I could take action, the second bully head-butted me from behind and pushed me forward. Simultaneously, his brother hip-checked me back into the pond.

The map and berries went flying and my whole body went under. I panicked, but tried to paddle my paws up to the surface of the water. Seconds later, I really freaked when one of them jumped on top of me. My head went under again. He was holding me down. I didn't have the strength to dog-paddle out from under him, so I tried to stand upright on my hind legs.

The bullies were so much bigger and stronger, and I was weak from a lack of food. The one thing I had going for me was my speed. When I stood upright, the pond wasn't as deep, so I had leverage and the bully slipped right off of me.

SPLAT!

When he fell back, his brother went down into the water with him.

I squirmed away from their paws, headed toward the edge of the pond, and climbed out onto land.

Back on all fours, my paws raced across the weeds in search of my brother and Joey.

I wasn't in the clear; I heard the growls of the bullies, letting me know they were chasing after me.

Seconds later, one of them caught up to me and jumped onto my lower back. He clasped his paws around my body and wouldn't let go.

I yelped and heard a loud pop at my hip. The pain was immediate.

He held onto me for a long time. I twisted and tried to get away. The pain got so bad, I finally howled out in agony. It was so loud I sounded like a wolf.

Up ahead, I saw my brother running back through the gate, trying to get to me. I wanted to yell at him, to make him stay away, so he did not get injured too.

But then I heard the powerful barks of Brutus and felt a glimmer of hope. He broke out of the chicken coop and was coming for me, too.

I howled again. It was so loud the noise scared the bully. He backed off, which gave me the chance to escape. I almost reached my brother when the bullies charged again.

This time, Brutus came out of nowhere. He placed his massive lab frame in front of me and blocked them from getting close. He growled like I've never seen him growl before. The dog trainer taught him to be mean, too, and the bullies knew it.

"Run," Brutus yelled to us.

Number four and I ran toward the gate. Once we reached the other side, we were panting and gasping for air.

We closed the gate behind us so the bullies could not come charging through. When we turned around to celebrate our freedom, Leroy Jones was waiting and grabbed us both by the fur on our necks.

"I told you there's no escaping Leroy Jones."

Chapter 24: Chicken coop is our new home

Leroy Jones did not return us to the porch. He locked us in the chicken coop and chained Brutus back up to the post. Now, it would be impossible for us to get food or water. I held onto my brother, relieved that we were still together.

"What happened to Joey?" I asked him, afraid of the answer.

If Leroy Jones discovered he was with us, he could have locked him up, or worse, he could have broken the wires that made the message work and pulled his stuffing out.

"Joey got away," my brother said. "Before I came back to find you, I told him to run and get to 111 Cranberry Lane."

I breathed a sigh of relief. "You should have gone with him and remained free."

He shook his head. "I was not leaving my sister. I thought those bullies were going to hurt you."

"They did hurt me," I said. "They jumped on my back and trapped me from moving. Something popped. It hurts a lot."

He put his paws around me. "I'm sorry we couldn't escape."

We curled up in the wood building and tried to get some rest. Leroy Jones and the dog trainer would probably have us on a freak show display the next day. I looked up at the sky and made a special prayer that Joey made it to his destination. I prayed for Brutus, too.

Neither one of us could sleep that night. We had nightmares all night long. Each time I closed my eyes, a dark shadow appeared, and suddenly, something was drowning me under water. I kicked my paws out and tried to break free. My brother draped his paws over me to make me feel safe.

Brutus was curled up outside the gate to the chicken coop, making sure the bullies couldn't get in.

"Try to sleep," he said to us. "The bullies won't get past me."

I still kept my eyes open and my ears alert, watching and listening.

Somebody must have been listening to my prayers this time. The following morning, there was a lot of action and noise going on outside the gate.

Chapter 25: We are free

It was early, still dark out, but the sun was slowly rising above the trees and shining into our new prison. I raised my head up when I heard a sound in the distance.

Sirens.

They got closer, and then I saw a reflection of blue lights twirling around in circles up in the trees outside the gate.

The bullies started barking, but Brutus remained quiet, with ears up.

I shook my brother to wake him up. "Something is happening," I said, scared but hopeful at the same time.

"Leroy Jones," a male voice said over a speaker. "This is the police. We have a warrant to search the premises. Open the gate."

With my good ears, I heard movement inside the house. Leroy Jones came bursting out through the door. He stormed across the porch and down the steps. Instead of going toward the gate to open it, he ran toward his field out back.

"He's making a run for it," I said.

Seconds later, there was a loud crashing noise as the police rammed through the gate. Uniformed men and women marched into the yard. Others rushed in from the back exit gate, too.

They must have known about the bad things happening out in the field. Leroy Jones tried to get away on his tractor, forcing the officers to chase him through the field. He was handcuffed and returned to the front. As they marched him toward the police car, he glared over toward the wooden building in the chicken coop, where we were hiding.

“You puppies better be here when I get back! You belong to me... nobody is going to stop me from capitalizing on those secret abilities of yours.”

He had a wicked scowl on his face when the police car drove him away.

Then a white truck with cages on the side pulled into the yard. Two men in tan work shirts and khaki pants stepped out carrying nets and a lasso to capture our doggy dad and the two mean dogs.

That's when I tore out of the wood building and clung to the fence of the chicken coup.

"Don't let them take you, daddy!" I cried, believing he was going to doggy jail. "I know you're good."

Brutus bent down to my level. "I'll be okay, little one," he said in his doggy voice. "Wherever they take me would be better than here. You take care of your brother. He's going to need you."

Just like my doggy mommy said. I tried to put my paws through the fence, but they were too big.

"Go on, little one," Brutus said. "Go back to your brother."

It took the animal control officers a while before they could catch the bullies. They growled, snarled, and tried to bite the lasso. Brutus stood still while they attempted to lasso him. When they realized he was not so mean after all, they just told him to come. And he followed. The uniformed men must have liked him. They let him ride up front with them.

When the truck pulled away, I heard the ferocious barking from the bullies, but it was losing my doggy daddy that hurt.

I was worried about him. It was the evil Leroy Jones who made him be mean. He didn't want to be. I didn't want him to go. I knew he was going to miss us as much as we would miss him.

"This might not have been our plan, sis, but we are finally free from Leroy Jones," my brother said.

"Yeah," I said, trying to look at the positive. "We survived. But where will we go? And how will we eat? Will they lock us up too?"

I wondered about that. And then I remembered what my doggy mommy said: I was smart. I would figure it all out.

Chapter 26: A Miracle

We remained inside the chicken coop while officers walked around the yard, collected evidence, and put up yellow crime scene tape. They didn't seem to pay any attention to us. After a while, they finished up and hopped into their cars, and drove away.

"Are they leaving us here?" my brother asked.

"I don't know. Maybe they don't know about us."

A short time later, another police car pulled into the yard. A young officer stepped out of his car and walked around the yard.

He ducked his head down under the porch and then he headed for the chicken coop. He opened the gate, walked inside the fenced area, and kneeled down to see us cowering inside the wooden building.

"There you are," he said, as if he had been looking for us.

His voice was soft. It was the first time we heard a human speak that wasn't mean. But we were still scared. I scooted closer to my brother.

"It's okay, you are safe," the officer said. "The mean man and dogs are gone. Nothing is going to hurt you."

Instead of reaching his hand in and grabbing us, like Leroy Jones always did, he remained where he was.

There was a gleam in his eyes, as if seeing us made him happy.

We haven't met any nice humans since we were born. All we had been exposed to was the evil Leroy Jones, the dog trainer, and his vicious bullies.

This uniformed man seemed different. He smiled a lot.

"I'll just wait right here," he said, sitting on the dirty ground. "You come on out when you feel safe."

"It must have been scary roaming around this yard with weeds and trash everywhere," the officer continued, trying to make us comfortable.

After a while, my brother was getting restless. He pushed me off of him and eased out. Before walking out into the open space, he peered back at me.

“He seems okay, little sis. Maybe he’ll get us some food, instead of scraps and berries we’ve been living on. C’mon.”

I still hesitated.

I kept my eyes on the officer as my brother approached him, ready to pounce if anything happened.

When my brother brushed up against the officer’s pant leg, I got anxious. I was sure he would kick him with his boot, just like Leroy Jones always did.

But nothing happened like I thought it would.

He kept smiling and put his hand out so my brother could smell his scent.

"Hello there," the officer said, allowing my brother the chance to get used to him before petting him.

I didn't come out all the way, but inched closer and kept watching. My brother was getting bolder. He went up on his hind legs, like I taught him to do, and put his paws on the officer's shoulder.

I held my breath when he picked him up. And then I heard my brother whimper, which in my current state of fear sounded like crying. Without hesitating, I tore out from inside the building, ready to come to his aid.

"I'm coming, big brother!" I yelled, ready to take on the big, mean police officer.

Chapter 27: Is he a believer

But I was wrong. My brother wasn't crying because of fear. The officer held him close, cooing at him as if he was a little human baby. My brother was quietly weeping with joy.

"C'mon little sis," my brother said, seeing that I was still nervous. "He likes us."

I eased closer to get a whiff of this new stranger. There were so many unfamiliar scents on his boots and uniform pants.

He must run into all kinds of strange people and animals during his workday.

It wasn't until he reached his other hand out that I relaxed.

"It's okay, little one," he said to me, using the same term my doggy mommy and daddy did. "I have someone at home who would just love to meet you two."

I just had to be part human for real, and not just in my imagination. Dogs don't feel the emotion in the same way humans do. And at that very moment, it felt like my little heart was going to burst.

He wasn't separating us.

This human, a police officer, came to save us from a horrible life. And now, he was talking about taking us to his home.

It seemed too good to be real. Could what we imagined in our stories come true? Were we going to stay with a good human family? Maybe I was still asleep, and this was just a dream.

That couldn't be. In my dreams, I am one hundred percent human. We drive cars. Ride bikes. Swim. Surf. Snowboard down the mountain slopes. Play sports. Read books. We can do anything.

"Let me put you down for a minute, little fella," the police officer said, placing my brother down next to me.

"Stay right there. I'll be right back. Oh wait, you're just puppies. You probably don't understand a word I'm saying."

I thought that was funny. He didn't know I was part human and understood everything.

He stood up, walked to the back of his police car, and opened the back. When he returned, he carried a large cardboard box. He placed it on the ground, picked up my brother, and placed him inside. My brother went willingly and his head popped out of the top.

When he tried to pick me up, I scooted back away from him.

I wanted to trust him, wanted to meet the person at his home who would like to meet us. I wanted it to be real.

But I was still scared, and my hip hurt. I was afraid if he picked me up, I would yelp. Then he might leave me, thinking I wasn't worth the trouble.

They took away our mother, father and brothers. It would take a long time to forget that and trust another human.

"Okay, little one, you're still unsure," he said. He picked up the box with my brother, walked to the passenger side of his police car, and set the box on the seat.

He stood by the car door and watched me. While we stared at each other, he seemed to sense something about me. He started talking to me as if I was a human.

Does he know?

"I know you're scared," he said. "I'll tell you what we're going to do. We'll go to the pet store for food, doggy bags, toys, and other stuff. Then we'll go to my house, where you'll meet Tara. She's been talking about rescuing a puppy for months now. We will be foster parents. She'll be so excited to see there are two of you. Won't that be fun to see the surprise on her face? The only reason I need the box is so that you don't get hurt with all my work equipment in the car?"

Was the officer a believer? Did he know we were part human?

"Come on little sis," my brother yelled from inside the box, getting impatient. "It will be our first real adventure."

I cocked my head to the side and sized up the police officer one more time. He seemed amused by that. We finally came to an understanding. Besides, he said he was getting food. My brother was getting skinny like me. He needed to eat. He's supposed to grow big, like our doggy daddy.

When I finally allowed him to pick me up, it was painful. But I tried not to cry. The mean doggy hurt me more than I realized.

The police officer didn't place me in the box right away. He held me up so that my face was in front of his, my paws dangling with no way to escape.

"You're going to love Tara," he said. "And she's going to love you. I promise." Then he gently lowered me into the box with my brother.

Once the car door closed and he was sitting in the driver's seat, my fear took over again. I wrapped my paws around my brother and mentally prayed we were going to a better place, like he promised.

Let's go to the pet store and get you some food.
POLICE
Come on, sis. He likes us.

Chapter 28: Stores and more humans

This was our first car ride. As adventures go, I would say it was a dud. The motion and constant humming of the police radio lulled us to sleep in the box.

When the car parked and the engine shut off, I was immediately awake and nervous all over again.

The officer picked up his phone, spoke into it for a moment, and then stepped out of the car.

Was he going to leave us alone?

No.

He walked around to the passenger side and opened the door.

“This is probably your first time in a pet store, so it will be scary, with all the smells and the noise. But there’s nothing that can hurt you.”

I like how he talked to us as if we could understand. My brother was too busy looking around, distracted as usual.

The officer picked up the box and carried us inside.

He was right; it was overwhelming. I could smell different animals and pets, rodents too. And some of the food smelled gross.

I could also hear everything.

It was scary. The sounds were all so new to me. My ears were always more sensitive to noise than the other pups, but it was like an orchestra of sounds all at once.

I heard human voices. There were squeaking sounds from the hamsters and guinea pigs playing in their cages. A telephone ringtone buzzed somewhere in the back. And I could hear a customer walking her pet down the aisles trying out different toys.

They let you try the toys?

The noises confused me. I was so used to hearing mean voices from the humans we lived with. These voices sounded... happy.

"Do you have puppies?" a young female at the cash register said as she hurried over to see what was in the box.

"Yes, but be careful with them," the officer said. "I just rescued them from an abusive home. I don't want to scare them or hurt them."

"Oh my God!" the teenager said, cooing over me and my brother. "Who could hurt puppies?"

"You'd be surprised," he said. "There are some not-so-nice people out there."

For the first time, I could hear the anger in his voice, and I could tell how much it bothered him.

"Can you help me?" he said to the girl. "My wife and I are going to foster them. I need healthy food, bowls, and anything else I might need for new puppies. I don't know how old they are. And they're going to need grooming. Aside from the filth, they smell like a skunk."

I smiled at that. It was the skunk plant that saved us from the bullies.

"Well, if they've been neglected, you'll definitely want to take them to the vet," she said. "And they'll need shots."

I freaked at that. Shots? Whoa, no needles for me, thank you very much. I ducked back down into the box.

For the next hour, we followed her through the store while he loaded up his cart. I think he bought half the store. Most of it was toys, bones, and things for us to chew on. He bought a crate and two beds too.

I knew he was serious about taking us in when he picked out a collar for each of us; one blue and one pink for me.

"We can't get tags made yet," he said to us as if we were expecting it. "Tara is at home picking out names."

I looked into the officer's eyes. He was serious. I wanted to put my paws around my brother and squeeze, but that inner voice kept holding me back.

"See, it's going to be okay, little sis," my brother said to me. "Somebody wants us so much, they are going to give us names and buy us tags."

I wanted to believe it. I imagined it for so long, but life didn't work out that way for us so far. No matter how much I told my brothers to believe, bad things kept happening. And now most of our family was gone.

My brothers were usually the negative ones, and now I was the one who was worried. I promised our doggy mommy I'd take care of them. It was my job, and I failed. Of course, I worried.

After spending a fortune at the store, and then watching us get bathed and blow-dried, the officer said it was time to go meet Tara, so we piled back into the car.

Chapter 29: What's not to like

During the drive, the anxiety reappeared. I looked at my brother. "What if he's wrong? What if she doesn't like us or only wants one of us?"

My brother smirked at me. "That won't happen. Besides, what's not to like?"

I pouted. "Easy for you to say; you're suddenly Mr. Happy-Go-Lucky. I'm the serious one who can't let go of the bad stuff."

"Well, just remember who did the bad stuff and who saved us."

I peeked out over the box.

The police car pulled into a private community with cute cottages lined up along the street.

The car took a few turns, and then he finally pulled into a driveway. I could hear the waves of the ocean. After getting dunked in the pond by the bullies, the water scared me. And there were voices, too, laughter... and other dogs.

Oh, no!

Other dogs...

We had never been around other dogs, other than our family and the bullies.

I scooted into the farthest corner of the box as if that could stop anyone from grabbing me.

The car door opened. The officer grabbed the box and placed it down on the ground.

Nothing happened right away. Then curiosity got the better of us. My brother and I got up on our hind legs and put our paws on the edge of the box and peered out.

"Oh my, they are adorable," a female gushed. I assumed it was Tara, but there were other people there, too.

A group was sitting by a fire pit. A couple of them had dogs lying next to their seats. Some of them were big. Other dogs were lying on beach chairs.

The woman who spoke walked toward us with her hand out. My brother slobbered all over it. I worried that would get him in trouble. Leroy Jones was always irritated with us. She didn't get annoyed. She laughed.

Suddenly, the weight from our upper bodies caused the box to tip over and we fell onto the soft ground. It wasn't mud, dirt, or weeds, like the yard we lived in. It was soft underneath our paws.

It's beach sand; I heard someone say.

The police officer leaned over and picked up the box.

"Be careful, they've had a rough go of it," he said to the woman.

"How horrible," she said, and I could tell she meant it. "Well, you're safe now."

I liked her voice. I was hoping she would like us, too.

She leaned down. My brother started showing off rough-housing with her.

I remained quiet and just watched.

Another dog walked up to us.

“This is Chloe,” Tara said. “She is a Shih Tzu.”

She was smaller than me, and I was the runt.

When Tara realized I was still scared, she gently picked me up and cradled me in her arms. She held onto me as if I was a fine piece of China that would shatter to pieces if I fell.

Tara likes me.
She named me
Belle.

"You're okay now," she said in a voice that sounded like an angel.

By that time, my brother was already wandering. Chloe was following him as they made the rounds to the other dogs.

Tara carried me over to those sitting by the fire. The officer followed my brother to make sure he didn't get hurt.

There were big dogs too, but they were gentle. Buddy is a big brown lab who treated us like we were his babies and his sister, Guinevere, is a yellow lab. I heard her mommy say she was a Queen. I didn't know what that meant, but she sat in a chair like it was her throne.

Chloe had a sister, Maddie, who was also small. She was almost black, like my brother.

"Everyone, meet Belle and Bubba; those are the names I selected," Tara said as she introduced us to all the humans by the fire.

They were all nice humans and friendly dogs. I couldn't believe this was real. It felt like we were living in a dream world.

Chapter 30: I have nightmares too

We stayed by the fire for a while, and then Tara took us inside to show us our new temporary home.

It was nice and clean. Nothing like the old house filled with trash and clutter that Leroy Jones lived in.

The first thing she did was set up a crate with water and food bowls just outside of it.

After she placed the two beds inside and added toys, my brother and I wandered in and looked around. After sleeping under a dirty porch our whole life, the crate was like a luxury home.

She put real puppy food in a bowl and filled the second bowl with water. Our hunger got the better of us. We rushed back outside and went straight for the food. As hungry as we were, we could only eat a little.

Our tummies felt sick.

Without me telling her, Tara seemed to understand. “That’s okay,” she said. “We’ll get something for those tummies to make you feel better.”

She rubbed the fur behind our ears. We soaked up the attention.

Nobody ever did that to us.

"How about we go for a walk and show you where you can go potty?" she said with a smile.

She attached a leash to our collars, and they took us outside.

Tara held my leash and the police officer—we learned his name was Jared—walked Bubba.

Belle and Bubba were the names they gave us. I liked them.

There were so many unfamiliar scents to get used to. First, they walked us into some short grass that felt good on our paws compared to the weeds we had been living in.

"This is where you go potty," Tara said.

I understood what she was saying, sniffed out a spot, and did my business. Bubba didn't seem to understand, but he peed where I did. He didn't go number two. I worried about that and hoped he didn't make a mistake later. He did that once in Leroy Jones' house. It was not good.

Another area was filled with pretty pebbles and seashells, Tara called them. Then we walked through the tallest grass I have ever seen. It was even taller than the weeds outside the porch where we were born.

"That's sea grass," Tara said, laughing when she noticed we were getting lost in it.

After playing a few minutes of hide and seek with Bubba, they walked us down toward the ocean.

The big, scary water...

All I could think about was the mean dogs trying to drown me in the pond.

Bubba wasn't scared. He kept pulling his leash forward and Jared followed, laughing.

I put the brakes on in the sand and stopped.

Tara sensed my fear.

She got down to my level and stroked me ever so gently. "You don't have to go anywhere you don't want to, Belle," she said, and she sat down next to me as if she completely understood. "We can stay right here and just watch your brother."

Bubba wasn't afraid. He was part lab, like my doggy dad. He went right into the water.

Jared took off his shoes, rolled up his pant legs, and let Bubba lead the way.

I watched, fascinated, as the waves came crashing to the shore. I thought for sure Bubba would run away from them.

But he wasn't afraid.

"It's fun, Belle," he yelled to me as another wave splashed him in the face. "Try it."

"I'm too scared," I said to my brother. "I keep remembering the pond."

"The mean dogs hurt you in the pond," Bubba said. "Tara and Jared won't let anything happen to us."

And almost as if he was trying to prove it to me, he stumbled. A gigantic wave crashed over his head and he went under. And just like that, Jared lifted him up out of the water to save him.

"See."

There are wonderful humans.

"Your brother is right," Tara said. "We won't let anything happen to you. What those mean dogs did to you was bad. That will never happen while you're with me."

I looked at Tara, stunned. "You understand what we're saying."

She smiled. "You can do anything when you believe."

It must be true. My doggy mommy said it. Joey said it. And now our new foster mommy said it. A human could actually understand what I was saying. I had somebody to talk to. That brought a warm smile to my face.

I got back to watching Bubba swim. Tara sensed I was conflicted, but didn't want to miss out.

"How about if we just walk closer and get our feet wet," she said. "I'll protect you."

I tried. But instead of leaping into the water like Bubba, I was fascinated by all the rocks.

I pushed a rock with my nose. It got buried in the sand. I started digging with my paws until I found the same rock. Tara was laughing, so it must have been funny.

After a while, Bubba was so exhausted from the water, Jared picked him and carried him home. Tara and I followed.

Before we went inside, I did my business in the short grass.

"You are such a good girl," she said.

It felt so good to hear that. Nobody ever praised me before.

When Bubba and I entered our crate, it didn't take long before we curled up and fell asleep.

And then the nightmares came...

Someone was trying to grab Bubba to take him away from me. My puppy legs kicked out. I bit at a big, rough hand. The hand smacked me. I rolled across the dirt, yelping...

Suddenly, I heard the smooth voice of Tara. She picked me up, walked over to the sofa where she had a pillow and blanket.

She was sleeping on the sofa to watch over us.

"It will be okay, Belle," she said in a comforting voice. "You and Bubba are here with me and Jared now. You're safe."

She positioned herself under the covers, so that I was lying next to her chest with the blanket over me as protection. I was so close, I could hear her heartbeat. She caressed me until I dosed off.

Not much later, I heard Bubba whining. He stood up on his hind legs, trying to get on the sofa with us.

I thought for sure Tara would get mad because the noise would wake up Jared. He had to get up early for work.

That didn't happen. She picked Bubba up and let him curl up with us.

"I have nightmares, too," Tara said, as if she understood everything we were going through.

Chapter 31: It was an accident

The first morning in our new home, I was still saying it was too good to be true. Bubba woke up early, even before Jared left for work. He didn't go potty before bed last night, so he went on the floor.

"It was an accident," my brother said when Tara walked into the room.

I hid in the corner. She would get mad this time, for sure. To my surprise, again, she laughed and blamed Jared.

"Jared didn't make sure you did your business before bedtime, did he?"

When Bubba had an accident on Leroy Jones' front porch, he yelled at him so loud the earth shook. Then he tossed him down the steps so the bullies could chase after him. Brutus had to save him.

We were stunned. Tara cleaned up the mess, sprayed it with something that made the room smell fresh.

"When you have to go potty, just go to the door," she said. "I'll know."

Bubba and I looked at each other, surprised. Tara never gets mad or yells at us.

Smiling as if it didn't happen, she grabbed the leashes and took us for a walk. We did our business. Bubba had to go again. She said: "good puppies", reinforcing our behavior. Then we went back inside and tried to eat. Our tummies still hurt, actually a lot, so we could only eat a little. We walked around our new home and explored while Tara took a shower.

"Bubba, look," I said to him when spying in the garage. "They have all the things we dreamed about?"

"What do you mean?" he said as he hurried toward me to have a look.

Tara and Jared had snowboards, a surfboard, bikes, and camping equipment. There was a bat and balls, and rescue equipment for Jared's job.

"This is going to be a fun place," Bubba said.

"As long as we're together," I said. I still secretly worried we would be separated.

When Tara finished getting dressed, she took us to a big, scary place. She said it was a doggy doctor who would make sure we were healthy.

We were terrified all over again. When we walked inside, there were other dogs there. Some of them were shivering in fear. Some were hiding under a bench. They were older than us, but they were just as scared as we were.

The doggy doctor was nice. She was like Tara, but she gave us bad news. Bubba and I were malnourished. We hadn't been eating right. And I had other medical and physical issues.

Somebody hurt my hip, the doggy doctor said. She did some tests and had me walk down the lobby to show Tara how bad it was. She said it could get worse as I got older. I would have to take medicine all the time.

Tara was crying when the doggy doctor told her.

“Who could do that to a puppy?”

I didn’t tell her a vicious guard dog jumped on me and trapped me.

I was sure they wouldn’t want to keep me now. Treatment was going to cost a lot of money. Then I wanted to bolt when I saw the needle. Shots. Yuck.

“It will be quick,” Tara said, trying to comfort me. “You won’t even feel it.”

She stood next to me and wrapped an arm around me. I forced myself not to cry. Bubba didn’t even flinch.

We got treats for being so good. All-in-all, I guess it wasn’t so bad.

When Jared got home, I was worried again. He and Tara were talking at the table and I just knew this was it. They were going to keep Bubba and send me away. Taking care of me would mean doggy doctor visits, or maybe trips to the animal hospital.

As usual, I got myself worked up for nothing.

Later, we ate dinner and sat by the fire with our new friends. Bubba and I even played with the other dogs. All of them seemed to sense they had to be gentle.

And then Maddie did the funniest thing; at least the humans thought so. I was a little scared. She got up on top of Buddy's head and tried to wrestle him. She was little, and he was huge—as big as my doggy daddy.

I didn't know why the humans were not scared, but I heard them talking. They said Buddy was always gentle to the little pups. It was so funny. Buddy just let her do it until the parent yelled at Maddie.

It wasn't really yelling though, because she was laughing at the same time.

When Leroy Jones yelled, the earth shook, and we would run and hide. I was seeing the difference.

These were wonderful humans and friendly dogs.

Chapter 32: Growing up and getting bigger

As the days passed, Bubba and I were still with Tara and Jared. They didn't send me away, and we were growing by leaps and bounds.

Jared worked a lot, so taking care of us was up to Tara. She worked on the computer at home, but always made time for us.

Since we were malnourished, she made food at home to help us get better. Boiled chicken with grain rice, vegetables, blueberries and strawberries. She made sure we drank lots of fresh water and gave us vitamins. We were finally getting healthy. Even though I still had my hip issue, I filled out so much that my paws looked and sounded like padded furry slippers when I walked across the floor.

Tara made sure I took the medicine to help me with my injury. Some days I didn't notice it at all. Our tummies were all better, too.

She taught us to play ball, Frisbee, tug-of-war with a rope. Bubba swam in the ocean almost every day. He even tried the body board in real life. I was still afraid, so I dug for rocks. Some days I was hot from running, so I would lie down on my belly to cool off. But I still shied away from going in deeper.

The nightmares didn't go away. Tara said they might never go away, but she helped me through them. She seemed to understand what I was going through. She and I would sit by ourselves, sometimes, while Bubba ran through the waves. We would just talk. She seemed to accept that I was part human. She told me she had a terrible childhood too. We both learned how to overcome our obstacles.

When Jared was home, he would get out the t-ball bat and hit tennis balls. Bubba and I would chase them. I would return them, drop them at Jared's feet and run deep for another. Bubba would get bored. Sometimes he would just try to take them away from me. But, I always won, because I could still use my thumbs.

Jared told me I was a natural athlete. Bubba was good too, but he liked the water more. Sometimes, when he went after the balls, a seagull would fly overhead, or a squirrel would be out looking for nuts and he would get distracted.

When it was time to play ball, I never got distracted. Tara said it was amazing. She could watch me chase balls all day long. Said I could have been a center-fielder, whatever that meant.

Some days, I suffered after playing too much ball, but I didn't want to stop. When it was cool at night, I could barely walk.

I had to go to the doggy doctor a few more times. They said the hip problem wasn't going away. It was something I would always have to deal with.

I heard Tara and Jared talking again. Bubba was bored, and biting on my paw, wanting to play. But I wanted to listen.

Jared was worried that I would make my hip worse with my constant playing.

"Jared, you see how happy she is when she's playing ball? After everything these pups went through, we can't take that away from her. She knows when she needs to rest."

"That's true," Jared said. "She stops now and then to take a break, and then returns the ball when she's ready."

"I swear she's more than part human," Tara said. "Watch her when you tell her to get the bat and ball. She knows exactly what you're saying. She can always find the same rock when the waves bury them in the sand too, even though there are dozens. And she always knows when one of her tennis balls is missing."

Jared laughed. "I noticed that."

"She would make a good search and rescue dog if they didn't hurt her hip," Tara said.

My ears perked up. What is a rescue dog?

Jared looked over at me, as if he was studying me. My head was bobbing from side to side, listening and trying to understand, while Bubba continued to bite me. Jared laughed when I pawed him in the nose to make him stop.

I wanted to hear more about search and rescue, but I didn't like where the conversation was going.

"Her hip issue could be a problem," he whispered, as if he didn't want me to hear. But I did.

"She also hates the water. Bubba might be good, though."

"Take him to work with you and try him out," Tara suggested.

Jared thought about it for a minute. "We've been looking for more dogs to add to the team," he said. "He's growing by leaps and bounds. And he loves the water. I'll give it a shot."

My heart deflated.

Stupid hip issue.

I just knew search and rescue would be fun, and I was going to miss out. I was happy for Bubba, though.

Chapter 33: Bubba Goes to Work

Bubba started going to work with Jared, and I stayed home with Tara. We played ball. Walked by the ocean to dig for rocks, and I sat by her chair while she worked on the computer. She thought I was sad because Bubba was gone.

No. I was sad because I couldn't do search and rescue, but I also missed the rest of my family. One day, I finally told her about my doggy mommy and daddy and my brothers. She hugged me and said she would try to find out where they were and make sure they were okay. I didn't want to get my hopes up. But if

Tara said she was going to do something, she would.

Bubba came home every day and told me about his training. I admit it; I was envious. He got to meet other police officers and K-9 dogs.

In training, they went swimming and hiking. He got to dig through big piles of dirt and rubble, looking for people who pretended to hide. Next week, they were going on a boat ride to look for victims of a pretend crash, teaching them how to do water rescues.

I only felt worse when Jared bragged about Bubba's accomplishments. When he saw my sad look, he reminded me I was smart and talented, too.

"I know you would be good at rescue, Belle," he said. "I'm just afraid you'll hurt your hip. And you don't like the water."

The more I heard them talking, the more I wanted to do it. And I knew I could, as long as I believed.

I was shy of the water because of what the bullies did to me. Maybe I could overcome my fear and show Jared I wasn't scared.

From that moment on, I was determined to prove it. On our walks, I joined Bubba and went deeper into the water instead of stopping to look for rocks. I let the waves go over my head and forced myself to not be afraid. Jared noticed, but he was still worried about my hip. Each time, he would rush over to see that I was okay.

My plan wouldn't work if he kept focusing on my injury. I had to work harder to get him to notice.

Then one night, we were all sitting around the fire pit and I got an awful feeling. I kept hearing something, but couldn't see it, and no one else seemed to notice.

The noise became so loud it hurt my ears and I whimpered.

"What is it, Belle?" Tara asked.

I stared at her, which is what I usually do when I want to alert her.

"You hear something?" she said as she scooted to the edge of the seat and looked around.

I put my paw on her knee to let her know this could be an emergency.

Tara always paid attention when I reacted. She knew how good my hearing was and sensed something, too. After attaching my leash, we walked to check things out. I led her toward the ocean. We couldn't see anything, but I could hear it.

The closer we got to the water, the louder the noise became. We looked in both directions.

"Oh, no!" Tara suddenly yelled out.

And I saw it too. Somebody had been fishing near a floating dock. They left their fishing pole positioned on the sand. A Great Blue Heron, which is a tall bird that hunts for prey in shallow water, was caught in fishing wire that wrapped around a lobster trap. The lure was stuck in its wing. The ocean waves kept pulling the Heron under and it couldn't get away.

Right then, all I wanted to do was help the bird. I jerked so hard Tara lost control of the leash. Forgetting my fear, I raced toward the dock and down to the water where the Heron was agitated.

It wasn't too far out, but deep enough where I had to face the waves when I jumped in. They kept crashing over me, pulling me under, but I forced my paws to paddle. I was stronger now and wanted to succeed. I just wanted to save the bird.

When I reached the Heron, it was trying to flap its wings, but couldn't. It kept going up and down in a frantic move and twisted from side to side. A wing was stuck in the metal wire. It had to hurt. There was a lot of blood.

I have always been good at holding stuff with my paws. I held onto the bird to calm it down. It pecked at me, but I ignored the pain. I knew it was just scared. Then I used my sharp teeth and tried to bite through the wire.

But it was taking too long, and the Heron was getting more agitated.

Tara was right behind me, screaming for Jared. Then I noticed him and the other humans running toward us.

Seeing me in action, the men realized the problem. They rushed into the ocean, grabbed tools from their belts, and started cutting away the wire.

Their appearance made the bird even more afraid, so I kept holding it and talking to calm it down.

Finally, they freed the wire, so I let go.

At first, the Heron just flapped its wings up and down and kept splashing water at me.

I thought it was mad.

“The Heron is saying thank you,” Tara said.
I observed and realized that was how it communicated.

“You helped me overcome my fear of water, so thank you, too,” I responded to the bird.

He seemed to understand. Its wings flapped one more time, and then its long neck tucked inward toward the body, and the Heron flew away, probably to find its family.

I understood how it felt. I still missed my doggy mommy and daddy, and my other brothers.

When I returned by Tara's side, she kept praising me and telling me how brave I was.

Bubba hugged me, too. "You have always been the brave one, little sis," he said, "even if you are a half-pint."

I laughed, because I was no longer the runt. We were now close to the same size, and I had bigger paws.

When we returned to the fire pit, everyone was gushing about my abilities. If it weren't for me, the Heron might not have survived.

Tara held me close and said I was a hero for saving it.

Jared must have thought so, too. The next day, he told me I was going with him and Bubba. I was going to train for search and rescue.

I was so excited I even let Bubba wrestle with me.

EPILOGUE

Bubba and I have learned a lot since the day we were born underneath the porch. Everyone deserves to grow up in a home where people will take care of them; children, puppies, and even a teddy bear that belongs to a little girl.

We couldn't make Leroy Jones or the dog trainer care for us, but some of our doggy wishes finally came true. We're being fostered by humans who love us, and now we're training to be search and rescue dogs. I couldn't have imagined a better life, and hope it can become our forever home, soon.

We still have a few more wishes to fulfill. Tara is searching for our doggy mommy, daddy, and brothers to make sure they find safe homes, too.

Later tonight, Jared and Tara are taking us for a drive to see our friend Joey, the army bear. When I told Tara about him, and how he was trying to get back to Hayden at 111 Cranberry Lane, she already knew the entire story. Turns out, it was Joey's owner who got the police to show up at Leroy Jones' house after Bubba and I were recaptured. The police were told there were some illegal shenanigans going on in the field, but there were also puppies being abused. That's when Jared showed up with the cavalry.

And that brings the story back to how we came to be search and rescue dogs training to save others in a pretend boat accident.

* * *

We continued dog paddling toward the victims. By the time we reached them, the smoke and flames from the boat were blowing over their heads. They were scared, but our presence helped to calm them so we could do our jobs.

Our focus was to guide them toward the inflatable so officers could get them back to the dock where paramedics would be waiting.

Using our upper paws, Bubba and I placed the flotation devices around our respective victims to help them stay above water.

Nudging the throw bags toward them with our snouts, we urged them to grab a hold of the rope. They were weak and wouldn't be able to hold on for long. Bubba barked to alert we were ready.

When the officers started pulling on the ropes, we paddled alongside and guided them to the boat.

“Good job, you two!” Officer Jared shouted with pride when we reached the inflatable.

He and the second officer helped us all into the boat and checked the victims for injuries.

Meanwhile, the fire boat arrived and was putting water on the flames. Locals had gathered to watch the scene and were now clapping and whistling.

A female news reporter spoke into a microphone as her cameraman filmed the scene:

"This is local news reporting from the marina, where we just witnessed the heroic actions of two dogs!" she said, almost as if she couldn't believe it.

"Yes, you heard that right. Two dogs jumped into the water as a fire burned out of control and helped two victims get to safety in a live-training exercise!"

A local yelled, "Those are some well-trained rescue dogs you have there, officers!"

"They're heroes!" said another.

"They sure are," Officer Jared said. He looked over at us and winked.

Bubba and I settled into our positions on the inflatable as it headed back to meet the paramedics. At that moment, I remembered what my doggy mom said to me before she was taken away: “Girls can do anything”.

I glanced over at Bubba and smiled. “Boys can do anything too, as long as we believe.”

CR HIATT writes action-oriented stories with strong female characters as the heroes that were inspired by reality.

The daughter of a military veteran, CR grew up in a small town where she became an All-American athlete. She knew early on that she wasn't cut out for the nine-to-five types of jobs – her tendency to daydream about adventures often got in the way. Being the daughter of a Navy Veteran, she did what was necessary to be secure. She pushed those dreams aside and settled on working in the entertainment legal field. When those dreams invaded her world once again, CR finally gave in and set out to create her own adventures.

The journey started after she interviewed big city detectives and then talked with victims from cases they investigated. In those interviews, she was introduced to crimes of stalking and human trafficking. Those subjects became the plots for her series featuring Katie Parker. The novels are works of fiction based on actual events, only you can't help but wonder while reading the books which parts are true.

This latest work is a children's fantasy adventure entitled: The Great Puppy Escape - The Adventures of Belle and Bubba. The tale was created and written using the reality of her own Golden Retriever's early life before she was adopted. The book is for children, mostly middle-grade, but anyone who loves dogs and adventure will enjoy the story.

During her downtime, CR enjoys renovating houses; riding e-bikes with friends, and playing with her Golden Retriever, Annabelle. She is a huge supporter of the military and first responders.

Thank you for purchasing and reading The Great Puppy Escape - The Adventures of Belle and Bubba.

Readers and word of mouth are crucial to an author's success. If you read the story and enjoyed it, I would be honored if you would consider leaving a one or two-line review on Amazon.

Thank you so much.

For more information on CR HIATT, or to receive updates on upcoming releases, check:
http://writercrhiatt.com/
https://www.facebook.com/CRHIATT
https://twitter.com/CR_HIATT
authorCRHIATT@gmail.com.

www.ingramcontent.com/pod-product-compliance
Lightning Source LLC
Chambersburg PA
CBHW070834020826
48982CB00019B/1093/J

* 9 7 8 0 9 7 6 1 4 2 3 9 3 *